P9-CEZ-831

D0014991

Dear Reader,

When does the history of America really begin? Some might say the landing of the faithful Pilgrims at Plymouth Rock. Or the Boston Tea Party. Or the ratification of the Constitution.

But the history of people on this land reaches back much farther than that. Great nations stretched across the continent long before the first Europeans arrived, building earth mounds that rivaled the Pyramids of Egypt, roads that surpassed those built by the Romans, and developing some of the most sophisticated agriculture and astronomy in human history.

Many of those people and cultures were lost as settlers swept in, claiming land and pushing the original inhabitants out. But the contributions of the indigenous people of America still affect the modern world today. Sadie has always loved history. And in this book, she learns even more about the history of the people who were here before Europeans arrived, what it was like when the two cultures collided, how those original cultures still thrive, and how all of that influences us today. Along the way, she learns how much all of us can discover about ourselves from exploring the history of others—and what surprises we find when we start to realize how deeply the history of others connects with our own.

Vera Dodge
writing as Carole Jefferson

Mysteries of Silver Peak

MYSTERIES
of SILVER PEAK

Instrument of Peace

CAROLE JEFFERSON

Guideposts

New York

Mysteries of Silver Peak is a trademark of Guideposts.

Published by Guideposts Books & Inspirational Media
110 William Street
New York, New York 10038
Guideposts.org

Copyright © 2015 by Guideposts. All rights reserved.

This book, or parts thereof, may not be reproduced, stored in a retrieval system, or transmitted in any form or by any means, electronic, mechanical, photocopying, recording or otherwise, without the written permission of the publisher.

The characters and events in this book are fictional, and any resemblance to actual persons or events is coincidental.

Acknowledgments

Every attempt has been made to credit the sources of copyrighted material used in this book. If any such acknowledgment has been inadvertently omitted or miscredited, receipt of such information would be appreciated.

Scripture quotations are taken from *The Holy Bible, New International Version*. Copyright © 1973, 1978, 1984, 2011 by Biblica, Inc. Used by permission of Zondervan. All rights reserved worldwide. www.zondervan.com

Cover and interior design by Müllerhaus
Cover art by Greg Copeland represented by Deborah Wolfe, Ltd.
Typeset by Aptara, Inc.

Printed and bound in the United States of America
10 9 8 7 6 5 4 3 2 1

Prologue

HE HAD ALWAYS PRIDED HIMSELF ON HIS SENSE OF DIRECTION. IN fact, that might be what had kept him from admitting that he was lost for the past hour—perhaps the last several hours.

But now, there was no denying it.

The sun had long since dropped behind the high ridge of the mountains that towered over him, and the last light was quickly fading from the pine forest that surrounded him. His horse still trotted on gamely, but he could tell that the animal was winded after the long day.

He was winded too.

They both needed food, water, a warm place to spend the night.

And a safe one.

He was a pioneer, so he'd laid his head in all kinds of rough places. He wasn't afraid to sleep under the stars, or to lay his head down amid the roots of a sheltering tree.

But he'd spent enough time catching rest in odd places to know how important safety was. A rube just off the train from out East might make the mistake of bedding down for the night in unknown territory, mistaking the grassy Colorado forest for a pleasant stopping place, the stuff of poetry.

But he knew better. The Colorado wilds were full of threats to a man and beast on their own, unprotected by the watchful eye and backing aim of companions. Even if they were able to get to sleep without anything to eat or drink, as soon as night fell in earnest, they'd be at the mercy of the bears and other creatures that prowled during the darkest hours.

Or perhaps they would discover the hard way that they'd wandered into the territory of one of the tribes that called Colorado home, either because their people had always lived in these mountains and woods, or because they'd been forced westward when settlers took possession of their lands.

He'd done business with the members of tribes before. Many of them were friendly. But still, he'd prefer not to have to meet one by surprise, in the dark—especially if he was inadvertently trespassing on their land.

His horse whickered wearily.

"I know, Blaze," he said. "We'll be off the trail soon."

He suspected Blaze knew just as well as he did that they were already off the trail. In fact, he'd been wondering for about an hour if he should have reined in the horse so sharply when it tried to venture down a mountain path to the left, rather than the right. He'd insisted the big beast follow his lead, and the horse had obeyed him reluctantly. But he was starting to ponder as to whether the old horse, which was just as familiar with the Colorado terrain as he was, had been right.

As the light dimmed again, and no familiar path or landmark emerged from the seemingly endless woods, his eyes started to dart from side to side, searching not just for a clue to a trail now, but for a safe shelter where he and his horse might last the night—a cave, or even some kind of shelter against a large rock, where they'd at least be protected from several sides by whatever might come after them.

The woods faded to genuine darkness, lit only by the silvery light of the moon and stars, before he found anything.

By now, the horse had slowed to a hesitant walk, careful to dodge each tree and branch as they loomed up from the dark.

To his knowledge, he had never had a hallucination before. But now the dark and the worry acted on him strangely: He heard the faint strains of music.

Rattled, he shook his head and reached down to pat his horse's flank, hoping that the touch of something solid and living would bring him back to reality.

But the music only got stronger. It was like nothing he had ever heard before, but it was still strangely familiar: the lilt of the Celtic songs his mother had sung him to sleep with as a child, but also oddly like the melodies he'd heard sung at the few tribal gatherings he'd attended.

Now it had become so distinct, he realized he couldn't be imagining it.

Someone was playing an instrument, deeper in the woods.

It didn't sound like the music of tribal celebration—there were no voices raised, no hum of a surrounding crowd, no drumming from a circle.

But whoever it was, they sounded as if they knew this stretch of woods better than he did. At least, they were a whole lot more comfortable than he was spending the night here. And it sounded like a single person—or a small group, one that might be willing to welcome him, or even give a bit of help.

He turned the horse's head in that direction.

They trotted toward the music through the night.

1

———

SADIE COULD NEVER HELP SMILING WHEN SHE WALKED THROUGH the doors of the Silver Peak Library.

Besides antiques, books were her favorite thing in the world, and for the same reason: Most of them were full of history. And to Sadie, that didn't just mean dry lists of names and dates. To her, history meant stories, of all kinds: tragedy, triumph, romance—and mystery. That was another one of Sadie's favorite things—puzzling to find the whole story from the handful of clues that an antique offered. It kept her mind sharp. And sometimes, it might just shed light on the way life was today.

Kimama, the librarian, greeted Sadie with a big smile. Then she turned the smile on Alice, Sadie's daughter, who had just followed Sadie into the library.

"Hi, Alice! And Sadie," Kimama said. "I'm so glad you could make it."

"Make it?" Sadie joked. "I'd like to see you try to keep me away."

Kimama laughed. "I have to admit, I have a soft spot for people who take that kind of interest in native history."

MYSTERIES of SILVER PEAK

From across the room, a young man, high-school age, came up to the counter. Sadie stepped aside, to allow him to do whatever business he needed.

But to her surprise, he stepped behind the counter, and took up a spot beside Kimama, a questioning look in his eyes.

"Well," Sadie said, "I thought I knew all the staff here at the library. But it seems you've got a new addition."

Kimama smiled at Sadie's obvious surprise. "James," she said. "This is Sadie Speers. She's an expert on antiques, and she's going to be helping us try to identify the piece that just came in for our Thanksgiving exhibit on native history."

James stuck his hand across the counter and gave Sadie's hand a hearty shake.

"And this is my daughter, Alice," Sadie said. "I may be the expert in antiques, but she knows much more than I do about native history."

"Nice to meet you," James said, shaking Alice's hand as well, with a shy smile.

Sadie liked him immediately.

"James is our new intern," Kimama says. "He's been doing an independent study at the high school on native history, and is helping out on our native exhibit as part of his assignment."

"How did you get interested in native history?" Alice asked.

"It's my history," James said. "I'm a member of the Ute."

Alice smiled. "Well, that's a pretty good reason..."

Sadie filed back through her own knowledge of Colorado history. "Their history in Colorado goes back thousands of years," she said. "And they lived all over the state."

James nodded.

"And beyond," Alice said. "The name of the state of Utah actually comes from the tribe."

Kimama nodded. "The whole western third of Colorado was once a Ute reservation," she said. "They're one of the three major native groups in Colorado that we're featuring in the exhibit: Ute, Navajo, and the Cheyenne and Arapaho."

"The Navajo in Colorado are mostly concentrated in the Four Corners region," Alice said.

"The biggest reservation in the country is there," James added. "Not in Colorado, but in Utah, Nevada, and Arizona."

"But of course," Kimama said, "you can't have a nation in that area without influencing Colorado, as well."

"And as I understand it," Alice said, "the Cheyenne and Arapaho didn't originally live in Colorado. They were forced here by the westward migration of settlers."

Kimama nodded. "That's right," she said. "But the plains tribes still had significant influence as they moved west. The whole way of life for the Ute people changed when horses were introduced."

"We became expert horsemen," James said with pride.

To Sadie's surprise, Alice didn't seem to be following the conversation. Instead, she was staring at something over James's shoulder, just outside. Then suddenly she dropped her gaze, pretending to intently study the list of the library's opening and closing hours, which some library staff member had helpfully taped to the counter.

When Sadie glanced over, she understood exactly why.

Spike Harris was walking through the front doors of the library to greet them, his longish salt-and-pepper hair hanging around his craggy but friendly face. He was smiling so wide, Sadie thought to herself, you'd think he'd just won some kind of lottery. And she knew that, in his book, he probably thought he had. His crush on Alice was more or less an open secret, although he'd never gone so far as to put his feelings into words.

"Alice!" he practically yelped as he reached the counter.

Alice gave him a guarded smile. There was no reason to dislike Spike. He played pretty much every stringed instrument you could imagine in the local bluegrass band, the Skylarks. He was great with the kids he taught at his own shop, the Silver Peak Music Emporium. And he was on good terms with just about everyone in town. But as far as Sadie could tell, he wasn't Alice's type. And so his obvious enthusiasm for Alice could make their encounters awkward.

"What are you doing here?" he asked happily.

"Kimama asked my mom to come in and consult on a piece that just came into the library," Alice said.

"For the exhibit on native history," Sadie said. "Good to see you, Spike."

"Hello, Sadie!" Spike said. He smiled at Sadie, but try as he might, he couldn't seem to focus his attention on anything but Alice.

"I'm working on the native history exhibit too," he said. "I'm teaching myself to play a native instrument."

"Since he seems to be able to play anything with strings, I thought maybe he'd be able to do something with this one," Kimama said.

"What kind of instrument is it?" Sadie asked.

"They don't know!" Spike said. "And I've never seen anything like it. But it still plays," he added. "And beautifully. It's got a very special sound, real pure, almost like a lute. As soon as I picked it up, it was like it wanted to teach me a whole new set of songs."

"I'm going to teach him some," James said.

"That's right," Spike said with a grin. "The Utes have done a great job of preserving their own music. James here is a musician himself. So he's been teaching me some of their songs. And I keep trying to get him to teach me some of his own."

"He writes his own songs?" Kimama said. "I hadn't heard that before."

James looked at Spike with a mixture of betrayal and pride at being revealed as a songwriter.

"He does," Spike said. "And they're good. Maybe the next generation of Ute kids will grow up listening to his songs."

Alice couldn't help but give Spike a genuine smile as she watched James perk up under this encouragement. And suddenly, it was Spike who looked like a proud teenager.

"That's actually why I invited you in," Kimama said. "To look at this instrument."

"I'm already intrigued," Sadie said.

"So are we," Kimama said, exchanging a glance with James. Then she looked back at Sadie. "You're familiar with our native history exhibit. I know I've seen you stop to browse it in the past few years."

Sadie nodded. "It's one of my favorite features of the library," she said. "And as a lover of antiques, I think the idea is just brilliant: to ask local people who have items relating to native history to put them on loan to the library for the exhibit."

"But you never had this instrument on display before, did you?" Spike asked. "I always make sure I spend a little time here every year before Thanksgiving, and I don't think I've ever seen it. And I think I'd remember it if I had."

"It is pretty remarkable, isn't it?" Kimama said with a smile.

"It's beautiful," Spike said. Then his gaze turned involuntarily on Alice, as if he couldn't say the word without thinking of her.

"Who did it come from?" Sadie asked.

"The Granby family," Kimama said.

"That's interesting," Sadie said. "I know many families in Silver Peak claim some native ancestry. Even the ones who don't," she joked.

Kimama raised her eyebrows wryly.

"But I'd never heard the Granbys mention any native connection," Sadie continued.

"They don't have native ancestry," Kimama said. "At least not that they know of. But, of course, all kinds of things wind up in the hands of all kinds of people, for all kinds of reasons."

Beside Sadie, Alice nodded.

"I wonder why they took so long to offer it then," Sadie said. "Your display has been a holiday tradition in town for years. Why this year?"

"Because I finally convinced them to share it," Kimama said.

"So you'd been trying before?" Sadie asked.

Kimama nodded. "Yes. Almost since the beginning. Candace Wilson, who is a daughter of the Granby family, serves on the board of the library, and I had to go over to her place once to work on some library business. The instrument was right there in their main room, displayed on a shelf. It was so gorgeous that I wanted to know everything about it. But she didn't know much. And she didn't seem to want to talk about it. So I just kept asking, as politely as I could, every year."

"Maybe this year, she finally figured out you weren't going to stop asking," Sadie said with a smile. "Unless she finally let you put it on display."

Kimama grinned. "Well, in any case, this year, she finally said yes. And it turned out to be a good year, because of James here."

James, who got less enthusiastic about being the center of attention the more the little crowd at the desk grew, ducked his head. "I don't know about that," he said.

"He's being modest," Kimama said. "But he was the one who gave us our first clue. He recognized what are clearly Ute markings on the instrument."

"A musician and a scholar," Spike said proudly, but this still didn't coax James to raise his head.

"Well, that should narrow things down," Sadie said.

"You would think so," Kimama said. "But as far as we can tell, the Ute didn't traditionally use this kind of instrument."

"Interesting," Sadie said, excited about the promise of a mystery.

"We used mostly drums, or notched sticks that worked as resonators," James said. He ducked his head again. "At that time, I mean."

"Today, he plays a mean guitar," Spike said. "I've heard him."

"Do you have any idea how old it is?" Sadie asked. "If it's a more recent piece, there would have been a lot of culture exchange as settlers moved west. Some members of the group might have started using instruments they bought. Or traded for with other communities."

"Not this one," Spike said. "I don't pretend to be an expert on antiques. Or native history. But I do know instruments, and this one is handmade, all the way. And I've got no way to prove it, of course, but if I were a betting man, I'd lay a big wager that it's one of a kind."

"I could believe that," Kimama says. "I'm not an expert, but I have seen a lot, and I've never seen anything like it."

"Well," Sadie said, "I've got to say, I'm curious. I can't wait to see it myself."

Kimama glanced at Spike. "You were just practicing with it in the back room, weren't you?" she said. "Would you mind bringing it out?"

"One mystery instrument," Spike said with a grin, "coming right up."

He loped across the library to the rear room that was off-limits to the public, where Kimama accepted deliveries and staged exhibits.

Kimama gave Alice and Sadie a rueful grin. "It's probably silly, my making him practice back there, instead of just letting him take it home, where I'm sure he'd be more comfortable. And it's not because I don't trust him. He treats that instrument like it's made of spun glass. Any museum curator would be glad to have him. But I just hate the idea of letting it out of the library. It was hard enough to get the Granbys to let it out of the house."

"That makes sense to me," Sadie said. "I had a piece on loan from a family once on display at my shop. I felt so responsible for it I had to resist the urge just to bed down on the shop floor each night, so I could make sure it was safe even in my sleep."

Kimama grinned. "So you know the feeling," she said.

Sadie nodded. "It's a lot of responsibility, caring for a family's history," she said. "And it sounds like this isn't just about a single family story. It's part of the history of the native nations. And how that affects how we live and who we are today."

"That's what I've been trying to make these exhibits about, anyway," Kimama said.

As she spoke, Alice drew in her breath. "Spike?" she said, looking toward the rear of the library.

Kimama, Sadie, and James all turned as one, to see Spike lurching up from the back room. His face was ashen, and his gait was so unsteady that he seemed to have sustained a blow. Sadie actually made a quick survey of the library, to see who might have attacked him. But aside from their little group, and a handful of patrons who were quietly flipping through books or using the library's computer bank, the place was empty.

So were Spike's hands.

"Are you all right?" Alice asked, taking a few steps toward him.

"Where is it?" Kimama demanded. "Where's the instrument?"

Whatever had happened to Spike in the back room, not even Alice's evident concern for him, which might have delighted him at another moment, could distract him from it.

"It's not there," he said.

Before he could say anything more, Kimama charged out from around the counter, heading for the back room. After a moment, the whole group straggled after her. When they filed into the small room, full of carefully labeled boxes and well-organized exhibit placards, Kimama stood in the middle of it, her hands on her hips.

"What happened?" she asked. "What did you do with it?"

"Nothing!" Spike insisted, his voice full of emotion and bafflement. "I did exactly what you always told me. As soon as I was done playing, I put it back in the case. Then I closed it and double-checked the latches. I left it in the place you chose for it, on the floor in the far corner, so it couldn't get damaged by falling, and would be out of the way of foot traffic."

Kimama looked hard at him. Sadie could tell that she believed Spike to be sincere. But it was also clear that her mind was working hard to figure out what in the world could have happened to the instrument, if Spike *was* telling the truth.

"You must have mislaid it," she said. "It has to be here. I've been standing at the front desk all morning. No one's taken anything that big out of the library."

Even more agitated, Spike went over to a dim corner, then returned with what looked like an old-fashioned mandolin case. It had fallen open in his hands to reveal a merry orange-colored velvet lining—but no instrument.

"I didn't mislay it," Spike said. "The case was just where I put it. But the instrument wasn't."

He laid the case down on the long table that dominated the center of the room, partially covered with neatly organized curatorial materials, papers, and supplies.

The five of them stared at it for a long minute.

When Sadie glanced over at Kimama, tears had sprung into her eyes. "How in the world—" she began.

"Wait," James interrupted. "Is that it? Over there?"

"Over where?" Kimama asked, pulling herself together instantly.

"There," James said, and pointed at what looked like the delicate neck of an instrument poking out from behind a tower of boxes.

"That's it!" Spike said. "That's it. Thank God."

He wasn't particularly religious, Sadie knew, but it was interesting how people recognized their need for God in tough moments—even if the need wasn't to ask for anything, but to give thanks.

Spike sprang over to the boxes, took the neck of the instrument gently in his hands, and then carefully, carefully inched the boxes away from the wall, to release the instrument from where it had been wedged between them.

As he did, his face fell.

"What?" Kimama said. "What's wrong?"

Slowly, Spike lifted the instrument for them to see.

Sadie's mind whirred with interest at the sight of the unusual design. It was shaped something like a medieval lute, but the neck was shorter and narrower, and strung with varicolored strings. The face was covered with an intricate pattern of native designs, as well as what appeared to be characters, perhaps from a language she didn't recognize.

But she didn't need to be able to read it, or be an expert on instruments, to understand Spike's distress.

The beautiful old instrument was almost split in half. The wood wasn't in splinters, but the whole face of it swung completely free from the back.

2

KIMAMA GRIPPED THE EDGE OF THE TABLE AS IF SHE FELT THE room beginning to reel.

"I can't believe it," she said. "This can't be happening."

With great care, Spike laid the instrument into the cradle of the orange-lined case. Watching him, it was almost impossible to imagine him doing the kind of violence that had obviously been done to the instrument. But, Sadie knew, people weren't always the same in private as they appeared in public. And as much as she liked Spike, he might have his secrets, just like anybody else.

"How could this have happened?" Kimama asked again.

"I don't know," Spike told her. "I'm just so sorry. I left it here last night, exactly where you said to put it…"

"And I locked up and checked the room before I left," Kimama said. "And you had stayed a little after hours to finish up what you were working on. So there weren't even any patrons left in the place then."

"Unless they were hiding somewhere," James said. "Do you think someone might have stayed after? In the bathrooms? Or in one of the reading nooks?"

"They would have had to dart around like a hero in an action movie for me not to see them while I was doing my last check," Kimama said.

"But it might have been possible?" Sadie asked.

Reluctantly, Kimama nodded her head. "I'll have to make a list," she said. "Of everyone I can remember coming into the place last night. But it was such a big group, it's not going to be easy. We've got a bunch of teens in these days, starting work on their final projects for the fall semester. And we had two elementary-school reading groups. All those kids. And all those parents."

As she was talking, Spike's eyes widened. And his face fell.

"Spike?" Alice asked.

His eyes dropped to the broken instrument before him on the table. "And there was someone else," he said.

"Someone else?" Kimama asked.

Spike nodded. "A few hours before I left," he said. "My buddy came by. He doesn't play with the band, but he loves old instruments. I knew he'd be into this one, so I invited him to come over."

"To the library?" Kimama asked.

Spike nodded.

"Into this room?" she said, her voice rising slightly.

Spike hung his head. "I didn't let him touch it," he said. "He just sat in the corner and listened. He gave me some real good feedback, on how to play when the neck is so narrow, and fretless. And he had an idea for a verse in the song I've been working out."

"When did he leave?" Sadie asked.

"A few hours before closing," Spike said. "I was excited. I wanted to work on some of the things he'd told me. Work on the song and work on how to play it. So I hung out for a while after."

"So he was gone well before closing?" Kimama said. "Did you see him leave?"

Spike nodded. "Yep," he said. "I walked out with him. It always helps me to take a break when I'm working on something creative. You know, walk around. Change it up a bit."

Kimama's sigh clearly signaled her impatience with discussing the creative process in the midst of an emergency.

But Spike didn't seem to be able to stop himself from talking. And as he went on, Sadie's ears pricked up. "I didn't even let him touch it," he said. "He just kept asking a lot of questions about it."

"What kind of questions?" Sadie asked.

"Oh," Spike said, looking at the ceiling as if the answers might be written up there, "he was real interested in where it came from. And how much the library paid for it."

"We didn't pay for it," Kimama said. "That's the problem. It isn't even ours, and now it's in pieces." The emotion in her voice was evident as she spoke.

Alice reached out to give her a comforting pat on the back.

"That's what I told him," Spike said. "And then he got real interested in what it was worth."

Kimama shook her head. "I don't even want to think about that," she said. "Something like this, if we're right about it being one of a kind..." She shook her head in despair. "It's priceless. It could take years of the library's budget to replace it. And even then, it would never be replaceable."

"What about insurance?" Alice asked.

"Of course I'll have to make a claim, but I don't know if our rider will cover something like this, or even how much value we could assess it as having. But even if it is covered, I am not looking forward to having to tell the Granbys that their trust in me, in the library, was apparently ill-placed."

"Well, we still might be able to repair this," Sadie suggested. "I know some experts in restoration who you'd swear were magicians. You may not even be able to tell the difference when they're done with it."

"Yes," Kimama said. "But I'm still going to have to tell the Granbys this happened. I can't just give them back a repaired instrument without alerting them to the damage."

"No," Sadie agreed. "Of course you're right about that."

"I can't believe this is happening with the native exhibit," Kimama said. "I came up with the idea for it before I even got this job. So much of our native history is still in the hands of individuals."

"That's always been sad to me," Alice said. "I remember being so excited as a girl to look for arrowheads along the riverbank. A friend of mine found one one summer, and we all hoped we'd be the one to find another—for years. I never thought of it as taking a part of someone else's history. But that was what we were doing."

"That's right," Kimama said. "And it's a big part of the story. So I wanted to find a way to bring some of the history to light, both the history of the artifacts, and the history of who has them now. And I thought it would be most interesting to do that by focusing on the artifacts in a single community. I didn't know how many Silver Peak would have when I started. The first year I only put out a general call, and I figured if I didn't get anything, I'd just fill in with more traditional displays about the general history of groups in the state."

"And that first year was a big success," Sadie said, hoping to encourage her to look on the bright side in the face of the current situation.

"It was remarkable," Kimama said. "I was able to get several dozen artifacts, both from native families and from the families of settlers. And after that, it seemed to take on a life of its own. Once people saw the first exhibit, if they had something at home, they couldn't wait to be part of it. People started to bring me things year-round."

"That's amazing," Alice said.

"Yes," Kimama said. "But bittersweet. I got used to seeing pieces I knew would have had deep value to a native group, brought into the library by someone who had just found it in a box in the basement. But at least they brought them in. And as they started to understand the bigger picture, some of them even worked to find a way to return them to the hands of native people. Many of them had just never understood the larger history that they are a part of. When they realized the pieces they had weren't just interesting trinkets from ancient history, but important relics for people who are still living, it changed the way they think."

"Some of the things I've seen you display are only a hundred years old," Alice said. "Mom and I have several antiques that date back at least that far. The jeweled hairpin my great-grandmother always wore on special occasions. A needlepoint garden my great-great-aunt stitched when she was on a boat crossing the Atlantic to come to America. I can't imagine our family treasures being in the hands of strangers."

"Then you have some idea how we feel," Kimama said. "But now *this* family's treasure has been lost," Kimama said. "I told them I would personally be responsible for it. I told them the library had never had any item in the native exhibition damaged before. Or even mislaid!"

"And that was true," Sadie told her. "That was true, when you told them. But even the most careful curator in the world can't control everything. I don't think anyone would have believed that someone in Silver Peak would try to hurt one of these pieces. They'll have to understand that."

"There's only one thing I'm sure they'll understand," Kimama said, defeated. "And that's that they gave me a wonderful piece on loan, and I'm returning it damaged. I just can't imagine who would do such a thing."

Sadie glanced at Spike. "What did you say your friend's name was?" she asked.

"Oh," Spike said, "Steven."

"Steven," Sadie repeated, filing it away for future use. "And what did you tell him when he asked how much the library had paid for the instrument?"

"Just like Kimama said," Spike told her. "That the library hadn't bought it. That it was on loan. Then he wanted to know how much I thought it'd be worth if someone did want to buy it."

"And you said?" Alice asked, picking up her mother's line of questioning.

"I told him I didn't know. A lot, probably. It's obviously a real special piece." He looked down at the broken instrument again, his face stricken all over at the sight of it.

"It sounds to me like he was pretty interested in the value of this instrument," Alice said to Sadie.

"Oh, he's had money on his mind recently," Spike said, rising to his friend's defense at the suggestion that he might have had something to do with the damaged instrument. "It's been a tough time for him recently. He works landscaping jobs all through the summer, and then he usually picked up work with a temp agency in Denver through the winter months. You know, holiday parties and such. But they broke up this year. So he's been trying to get something else lined up. And his wife's due to have another baby just after New Year's. So he's had reason to be thinking about money."

Sadie couldn't believe that Spike didn't realize his defense of Steven did more to establish a motive for stealing the instrument than to clear him of suspicion. But she knew that it could be hard to believe anything bad of someone you'd known for so long. And Spike obviously had a long history with Steven, and a lot of affection for him.

But Alice, it seemed, didn't feel the need to be as delicate as Sadie. "It sounds like he might have had a lot of incentive to come back after the instrument," she said. "Or hide here after he pretended to leave."

Kimama glanced at her, then looked at Spike.

He gave his head a vehement shake. "No," he said. "I walked him out to the street. And besides," he added. "Whoever did this didn't take the instrument. If Steven wanted to sell it, why in the world would he have done this kind of damage to it?"

Behind the group, the door to the back room swung open. Heads swiveled to see a teenage girl with straight brown hair, wearing a library assistant badge, standing in the doorway.

"Kimama," she said, then paused when she saw the serious expression on her boss's face. "Oh...I'm sorry, did I interrupt?" She started to back away. "I can just..."

Kimama stopped her with an impatient gesture of her hand. "It's all right, Marcia. What did you need?"

"It's just the food drive," Marcia said. "Someone came in with a bag of food, but all the big boxes are full."

"At ten in the morning?" Kimama asked.

Marcia shrugged.

"Did you drive to work this morning?" Kimama said.

Marcia nodded.

"Then could you make a run over to the Market? They're collecting all the drive food there. Just load up everything we've got and take it over."

Marcia nodded and attempted a second retreat.

"Wait," Kimama said. "Is there anyone at the desk?"

Marcia shook her head timidly.

Kimama shook her head, more at herself than at Marcia. "James," she said. "Would you please cover the desk while Marcia handles the food drive?"

James nodded and headed for the door.

As it thudded shut behind him, Kimama sighed.

"I'm just so sorry about this," Spike said. "If I could do anything to make it right, you know I'd..."

Kimama looked at him wearily. "I know you would, Spike," she said. "I've seen how you treat this instrument. I've seen people be less careful with precious crystal."

"Then how...?" Spike began.

"I don't know," Kimama said.

Sadie crossed her arms. "We'll find out," she said. "There must be some kind of explanation. And we'll figure it out."

"I guess we should make a report to the police," Kimama said. "After all, this is a crime." She looked almost shocked as she said the words. Sadie had some faint idea how she might. The library had always felt like a sanctuary to Sadie. It must have felt even more like one to Kimama. To think of it as a crime scene was jarring.

Kimama went out to the main desk, where Sadie waited for her to make the call before joining her.

"I spoke with Sheriff Slattery," Kimama said as she hung up the phone. "He's going to send someone over to have a look."

Sadie patted Kimama's arm. "That's good," she said. "We're going to get to the bottom of this."

"Thank you," Kimama said. Her face didn't brighten, though, even with Sadie's promise. "I just feel sick about telling Candace what happened. After all those years of requests. And all the promises I made."

"Well," Sadie said, "I guess we'd better get it over with, then."

3

"THANK YOU FOR COMING WITH ME," KIMAMA SAID, AS SHE AND Sadie pulled up outside the Granby house. The Granbys had lived in Silver Peak for as long as anyone could remember, and their house was located near Edwin's, in the neighborhood of charming Victorian homes that had once formed the heart of Silver Peak.

The Granby house wasn't the fanciest of these homes, but it definitely had its own character. Unlike most of the others, which featured neat wood siding, this one was brick, with tall, narrow windows and black shutters, as well as a slate blue roof. It would have looked austere, even severe, if not for the lacy pattern of filigree that ran along the roofline, giving the whole place the feeling of a grand old lady who has made just one concession to wear a fancy dress for a festive occasion.

Sadie's heart went out to Kimama as the two of them got out of the car and stood for a moment, looking up at the house. Sadie had some idea of what Kimama was going through. No one could spend years of their lives buying and selling antiques without knowing the sickening feeling of seeing a treasured piece broken. Sadie had opened packages she'd been looking forward to for weeks, only to find the things she'd ordered in unrecognizable pieces due to shoddy packaging and shipping practices.

And she'd also been responsible for damage to a treasure that had been entrusted to her. She'd promised to do background research on an heirloom vase for a client, but she asked to take it with her so she could check it more closely for any details she might have missed at first glance. Like Kimama, she'd treated the vase so carefully that Julie, her assistant at the Antique Mine, started to joke that she had a literal pair of kid gloves in the accessories cabinet that Sadie should perhaps wear while handling it.

But all that care had been undone in seconds, when a deliveryman, trying to be helpful, had barged in through the door, his vision obscured by his heavy load, and bumped into Sadie's worktable, sending the vase tumbling to the floor.

Unlike the instrument in Kimama's exhibit, that vase had been beyond saving, although Sadie had called in not one, but two expert restorationists in hopes that someone—anyone—might be able to undo the damage. But she still couldn't bring herself to throw the pieces away. It had been a sickening feeling, carrying them up to the house of her client as they rattled inside a box. Even on the doorstep, she remembered still trying to come up with a way to explain what had happened that didn't wind up with the vase in pieces in the box in her hands. Eventually, she realized she didn't want to change the story. She wanted to change what had happened. But nobody could do that. So she just told the truth as simply and directly as she could.

Her clients weren't happy, of course, but they were even kinder about the accident than she could have hoped. Still, even years later, Sadie could feel the sting of it. And from the look on Kimama's face, she could tell that she was feeling it too.

God, Sadie prayed, *please be with Kimama. I'm not even sure what she needs right now, but I know You know. Please give it to her, whatever it is. Please bless the Granby family for lending this piece to the exhibit. This is a hard moment, but I pray You won't just fix it, that You'll also bring something good out of it for everyone who is involved. And I pray,* she added at the end, somewhat mischievously, *that I'll get a chance to be part of the way You help her.*

By now, the two of them had reached the front door.

Kimama drew in a long breath.

Sadie patted her on the back, to remind her that she wasn't alone.

Then Kimama raised her hand to knock.

Moments later, the door was opened by a trim woman in her fifties, her straight blonde-gray hair in a stylish bob, her blue eyes bright and intelligent. As soon as she saw Kimama and Sadie, she broke into a welcoming grin.

"Kimama!" she exclaimed. "It's wonderful to see you! To what do I owe this pleasure? And Sadie too. Another one of my favorite people in Silver Peak."

Kimama offered a forced smile, and Sadie grinned back at Candace. A few years ago, Sadie had worked with Candace to help find just the right antiques to decorate a room for her mother-in-law, who was at the nursing home and felt comforted by having things around her that she remembered from her youth. The two of them had always enjoyed the consults, and they still stopped to talk with each other whenever they crossed paths around Silver Peak.

"Come in, come in," Candace said, gesturing for them to step across the threshold.

Sadie knew how much effort it cost Kimama to take that step. She trailed in behind her.

It was only when they got inside that Candace seemed to pick up on Kimama's subdued mood. "So what brings you here?" she asked again. "Is everything all right?"

"Maybe it'd be good to sit down," Kimama said.

Nodding, Candace led them through the entry hall into a cozy sitting room. It was small compared to the floor plans of some modern houses, but the windows were carefully placed to let in the morning light and the ceilings were tall and airy. The place was decorated with a mixture of family antiques, with some modern touches thrown in: a sleek lamp and a reading tablet resting on a table.

By the time the three of them took seats, Candace looked genuinely worried. "Please," she said. "I'm sure I'm being silly, but is something wrong? Is everyone all right?"

Sadie glanced at Kimama, who was still finding her voice. "Everyone's all right," she assured Candace.

Candace sat back in her chair, her face relaxing into another smile. "Well then," she said, "that's all that matters."

"It's the instrument," Kimama said in a rush. "It's been damaged. I know all the promises I've made to you, and I'll never be able to tell you how sorry I am. But I will do everything in my power to make it right. Absolutely everything. I hope you can believe that. And I hope…"

"Wait, wait," Candace said, holding her hands up, her brow knit in concern. "Damaged? What do you mean?"

"The back of the instrument has separated from the body," Kimama told her, as if reciting the details from memory.

"Is it repairable?"

Kimama hesitated, and glanced at Sadie, who jumped in. "I don't want to make you any guarantees," she said. "But the wood isn't splintered. None of the designs have been damaged. It appears to have split right along the old glue-line. Of course, we can't know anything until we talk to an expert. And they may not know anything for certain until they get to work. But based on my own expertise, if you want to call it that, I'm hopeful."

Candace sighed, and looked back at Kimama. "But how did this happen?" she asked.

"We don't know," Kimama said, her voice rising with frustration. "I never let it out of the back room in the library, which is where we keep all our artifacts for the staging. Nobody but staff is allowed back there. And Spike Harris, who with your permission had been using the instrument to practice the musical element of the exhibition opening."

Candace nodded.

"I knew it wasn't an ideal space for an artist to work," Kimama said. "But I wouldn't let him take it home. Because I was afraid something might happen." Her face twisted over the irony of this.

"And did he do something to it?"

"We don't know," Kimama said. "Because we don't know who did it. Spike had used it last night until after the library closed. I locked up after him when he left. There's a chance he damaged it and tried to hide it that night. But he seemed just as shocked as we were by the damage."

"He was very upset," Sadie agreed.

Candace took a deep breath.

"Again," Kimama said, "I can't tell you how sorry I am."

Candace let out her breath and shook her head. "I can see that," she said. "And please, don't worry anymore. Of course, I wish this hadn't happened. But I'm glad to hear it's not completely destroyed, and that Sadie even thinks there's a chance it could be completely repaired."

"I can't promise that," Sadie interjected. "I don't want to make any promises I don't know we can keep."

"Of course not," Candace said. "But my main point is that I know you did your best, Kimama. And I want you to know that, as important as that instrument was to my family, it's not more important to me than our relationship. You're an absolutely great librarian. And a wonderful person. I've been proud to work with you on the board. And this won't do anything to change that."

Kimama's shoulders relaxed as if a great weight had just slid off of them. "That's very kind of you," she said. "I'm glad to hear it."

Candace smiled. "But I'm still concerned to learn what happened."

"Of course," Kimama said. "That's my first priority. I'm very concerned about what happened to your instrument. But I'm also concerned that until we know who caused this damage, I can't vouch for the safety of all the other artifacts that have been lent to us for the exhibit. People all over town, and some from around the state, have lent us those pieces. Every single one of them holds some important key to the story of native people. But they also have meaning to individual families, just like yours. I've made the same kind of promises I made to you, to them. And if any more of them sustain any damage…"

Candace was no longer worried simply about the fate of her own instrument. Her instincts as a member of the Silver Peak Library Board were kicking in. "...it could be disastrous for the library," she finished for Kimama.

The librarian nodded. "Of course, we're insured," she said. "But the whole point of this exhibit is the fact that many of these items are priceless, and irreplaceable. The time that gave rise to them has passed, and much of the way of life they were a part of has vanished. If someone is deliberately sabotaging the exhibit, and continues to harm our items, we'd have more than a problem with finances, even if we could compensate the families. So much of what we do is built on trust, and goodwill, and the work of volunteers. We have to live up to the trust that's been placed in us. Otherwise we could lose far more than a few pieces in this exhibit."

Sadie could see the strategizing that made Kimama and Candace both so valuable to the board. But she wasn't convinced yet that they had a saboteur in their midst—at least one who was planning to strike again.

"Well, before we get too far down that path," she said. "I think we need to consider all the possibilities. And one of them is that whoever did this was only interested in *this* instrument."

Candace looked at her in surprise. "But why this instrument?" she asked.

"I don't know," Sadie said. "Maybe you can help us with that. Can you think of anyone who might benefit from any harm coming to it?"

Candace shook her head slowly. Then she gave a brief laugh. "It's such a strange thing to wonder about...," she said. "The thought had never crossed my mind before."

Then she shook her head again. "I can't think of anyone," she said. "I mean, I'll keep thinking it over. But as far as I know, everyone in the family is doing pretty well financially. It's just me and my brother. He's a lawyer, and so is his wife. They work in fraud cases, and they've always been very careful with money. They're not the kind of people to have gotten caught up in some crazy scheme. And their kids are all fine. Healthy, too young to get into much trouble.

"And in fact," she went on, as if she'd just thought of something. "You know what? I just remembered that the instrument isn't covered on our insurance policy."

"It's not?" Kimama asked.

Candace shook her head. "No," she said. "The last time we bought a home owner's policy, I tried to list the instrument. Not for too much. Just ten thousand dollars. But Billy over at the insurance company called me up and told me the underwriters were giving him a hassle about it. Said that if we wanted it insured in that range, we'd need to get not just one, but two appraisers. And both of them cost a pretty penny themselves. And like you said, Kimama, I finally realized we weren't going to be able to go out and buy another one if something happened to this one. So I just let it go without listing it as a specific item on the inventory. Nobody in the family would be able to collect on it, even if they did damage it deliberately."

"Did they all know that?" Sadie asked.

"I mentioned it to my brother at the time," Candace said. "And to my husband. But the policy is made out to me. I'd be the main one to benefit."

"What about anyone outside the family?" Sadie asked. "Has anyone else ever expressed any interest in the instrument?"

"Well...," Candace said with a smile. "There's Kimama."

Kimama tried give her a rueful smile in return, but it was clear that she still felt too sick about the situation to joke about it.

"Anyone else?" Sadie asked quickly, to take the focus off Kimama.

Candace thought for a moment. "No," she said. "At least, not that I can think of right now."

"Or anybody else who might feel they had some claim on it?" Sadie asked.

"Claim?" Candace repeated.

"Well," Sadie said, "it's a native artifact. So it didn't always belong to your family. Do you know the story of how it came into your family's hands? Was there anybody else involved in it? Someone who might think the instrument belonged to them?"

Candace's eyes widened.

4

———

CANDACE SIGHED. "I DID THINK ABOUT THAT," SHE SAID. "PERHAPS we should have tried to find the original owners, and give it back. I even asked a few people who came to the house and had some kind of background in native arts. None of them could ever place it easily, though. Maybe I should have tried harder to find out its history."

"Actually," Sadie said, "I was thinking of its history with your family. Do you know how it came to be yours?"

Candace's brow furrowed. "I don't," she said. "We've had it as long as I can remember."

"Did you ever ask about it?" Sadie pressed.

Candace's eyes lit up with a memory. "You know, I remember I did," she said. But then her brows knit again. "And my mother didn't tell me much about it. I got the feeling she didn't like talking about it. So I never asked after that."

"Do you think she knows something she didn't tell you?" Sadie asked.

"I couldn't say for sure," Candace said. "But it'd be worth asking. Do you know where she and Dad live? They're just around the corner. They bought a sweet little bungalow nearby when Clive and I got married, so they could still be near, but so that we could start a new life in the family house. I was just on the phone with her before you came, so I know she's over there now. Why don't you head on over and see what you can find out?"

"Are you sure it won't be a bother?" Kimama asked. "Especially if it's a topic she doesn't like to talk about?"

Candace shrugged. "Who knows if I even got the right impression when I was a kid? It could be that she was just in a hurry to get something else done, and I interrupted her with another one of my endless questions. Maybe if I'd just asked again, I'd already know something that could help us figure all of this out.

"And in any case," she continued, "the situation's different now. We need to find out everything we can, to protect the exhibit, and the library. I'm sure she'll be glad to help."

To Sadie's relief, Kimama looked significantly less worried while walking up to Candace's mother's house than she had to her daughter's.

"I really appreciate your going with me," Kimama said as they approached the brightly painted red door of a snug bungalow that was, just as Candace had promised, right around the corner. "I should have known Candace would be as gracious as she always is. But it sure helped to have a friendly face walking up to the place with me."

"Glad I could be there," Sadie said. "And I haven't bowed out yet. I'm still planning to get to the bottom of all of this."

"Well, maybe this conversation will help," Kimama said. "In fact, I probably should do this interview anyway, if only for the exhibit. I can have James write it up later, as part of the information that's displayed with the instrument. I was planning to bring in an expert to give us his opinion on it, but it's always good to have the connection to the local history."

"For some people in Silver Peak, that might actually be the most interesting part," Sadie said.

She'd seen it in her store, again and again: People couldn't care less if an antique had played some big role in a history they didn't know. But if it was a poster from a carnival that had been to *their* town, no matter how small, suddenly that was news. Sadie thought it was probably only natural to want to know how things affected the way you were living your own life, or how things had once been different in the place where you were. But she'd always been curious about the big story herself. And she didn't think a person could understand the history of just one place without understanding how it related to everything else.

Kimama raised her hand to knock.

A moment later, the door was opened by a stylish woman in her late middle age, wearing a pair of light khaki pants and a blue sweater, accented with a bright scarf tied at the throat. Her graying hair curled around a welcoming smile.

"Hello, Beverly," Kimama said. "I'm Kimama Temoke."

"Of course!" Beverly said. "From down at the library."

"That's right," Kimama said.

"And Sadie," Beverly said, with a nod at her.

Sadie smiled back. The two of them weren't exactly the same age, but they'd been in town long enough to get to know each other.

"Your daughter said you might have some time to talk with us," Kimama said.

Beverly swung the door open to usher them in. "Well, of course," she said, showing them in to a bright, neatly appointed sitting room just to the left of the entry. As they sat down, she clasped her hands. "Can I get you anything to drink?" she asked.

"Oh, thank you," Kimama said. "But I'm fine."

Seated beside her in a stuffed chintz chair, Sadie shook her head as well. But there was no stopping Beverly, who slipped out of the room, calling over her shoulder from the kitchen, which seemed to be nearby, judging by the sound.

"I'm afraid I'm not going to let you off that easily," she said, her voice raised to carry. "I've just baked a tray of chocolate banana cookies."

She came back into the room, bearing a pretty teal plate, stacked with cookies that Sadie could see were still faintly steaming.

"You wouldn't leave without at least trying one for me?" Beverly said, sitting down with a smile.

"Well, if you insist," Sadie said, taking one of the warm confections. It was even more delicious than it looked, with the unmistakable taste of banana paired with a rich dark chocolate. "These are wonderful," she said.

"I sampled so much of the batter that it's hard for me to know how the cookies turned out," Beverly said. "It's a baker's problem."

Sadie nodded. "I know a bit about how that goes myself."

"Now," Beverly said, leaning forward. "What brings you here?"

Faced with broaching the subject of the damage to the instrument again, Kimama was visibly uncomfortable. "Well," she said, "as you probably know, Candace was kind enough to lend the library a piece that's been in your family's possession, to be displayed as part of our Thanksgiving exhibit on native history."

Beverly still smiled brightly, but Sadie had a sense that something about her expression had just frozen.

"I'm afraid there's been some damage to the instrument," Kimama went on. "That's what we were talking about with Candace just now."

Now Beverly's expression distinctly clouded. "Damage?" she repeated.

5

"WE'RE VERY HOPEFUL THAT THE INSTRUMENT CAN BE REPAIRED," Sadie said. "But we were hoping that you might be able to help us understand its history."

Beverly's hand flew up in a dismissive wave. "Oh," she said, "that old thing. I don't know anything about it."

"It doesn't have to be an expert opinion," Sadie said. "Kimama's hired a professional to take a look at it. But we were wondering if you could tell us anything about its story in your family."

"I don't know anything about it," Beverly repeated. Her smile had now vanished. Sadie searched her face, wondering if she'd said something specific to annoy her. But Beverly didn't look annoyed. She looked scared. And a little defiant.

Sadie had a strong feeling that Beverly knew more than she was letting on, but she also knew that the best way to get at the truth wasn't to say that outright. "It's such an unusual piece," she said. "It's exactly the kind of thing that kids in my shop would go crazy about. Do you ever remember being curious about it as a kid? Did you ever ask your parents about it?"

At this, Beverly actually rose to her feet. "I'm sorry, ladies. I wish I had more time, but I've actually got to be somewhere shortly."

"Do you remember anything they ever said about the instrument?" Sadie pressed. "Or any of your other relatives? Do you remember anyone talking about it?"

But Kimama was already rising to her feet. "Of course," Kimama said. "Thank you so much for your time. And again, I'm so grateful to your family for the loan of the instrument."

Now, for the first time, Sadie saw annoyance flash in Beverly's eyes. "Of course," she said tightly.

"Well, let us know," Sadie said brightly as she trailed Kimama toward the door, "if you remember anything at all. Sometimes it's hard to think of anything right off the bat, but after a good night's sleep, or a long walk, you never know…"

Beverly didn't even deign to respond to this try with another "Of course." Instead she just followed them to the door, watched them go through, and then gave a single wave, so abrupt it was almost a military salute, as she closed the door behind them.

Kimama sighed as they went back down the walk to the car. "I'm sorry," she said. "I know you wanted to see if you could get any more information, but I just couldn't stand the idea of causing any more trouble in the Granby family. Not today."

"I can understand that," Sadie said. "But I wouldn't say it was a wasted visit. I think we found out something important."

"Really?" Kimama said. "Then you must have heard a different conversation with Beverly than I did. Unless you learned something from that chocolate banana cookie you ate."

Sadie shook her head. "Nothing, except that it was delicious," she said. "And I think you probably learned the same thing I did. It's pretty clear to me that Beverly knows something…"

"She just doesn't want to tell us," Kimama finished for her.

6

THE BELL OVER THE DOOR IN THE ANTIQUE MINE JINGLED merrily, then the door swung open into the store. Before it could thud shut, Sadie and her entire brood, Sara, Theo, and Alice, had all looked up from their various posts around the shop: Alice reading a book behind the counter, Sadie and her grandson, Theo, working very carefully to clean the dust from the space-age illustrations that decorated the covers of a box of old Tom Swift novels, and Sara furiously engaged in a texting conversation with one of her fourteen-year-old friends.

The figure in the doorway looked almost comically like a movie adventurer, wearing a loose white shirt and a canvas hat with a wide brim.

At the sight of him, Sadie left the box on the floor beside the bookshelf where she and Theo had been filing them, and stood, Theo right behind her. Alice glanced at her mother, as if looking for an explanation of who this stranger might be.

"Dr. Gramas?" Sadie asked.

The man doffed his hat to reveal a slightly balding pate over a bespectacled face. "Yes, yes," he said. "I see I've made it to the right place. Are you Sadie Speers?"

Sadie threaded her way through the aisles of the Silver Mine to meet him, then gave his hand a hearty shake. "Guilty as charged," she joked. "It's great to meet you. It's not every day that we have a nationally known expert on native history in the shop."

"Likewise, likewise," Dr. Gramas said. "I've heard from Kimama that you're a bit of an expert yourself."

"Well," Sadie said, "ask my family, and they'll tell you I can't even find my car keys half the time."

"I always tell my family that's actually the mark of a true expert," Dr. Gramas said, with a laugh.

Sadie introduced him to Theo, then Alice and Sara.

But although he smiled politely, his mind was evidently elsewhere. His gaze kept darting around the store, as if he was looking for something.

"You'd like to see the instrument," Sadie said.

Dr. Gramas's eyes lit up. "You got me," he said.

"We can't wait to hear what you think," Sadie told him, leading him to the back.

Theo and Alice both circled around Sadie's worktable, where the instrument sat. Sara trailed in behind them. Even she seemed to think it was an occasion that warranted a break from what appeared to Sadie to be an almost eternal virtual conversation.

"Here it is," Sadie said, gesturing toward the table.

At first, Kimama had been reluctant to let the instrument out of her sight. But on reflection, she and Sadie had both decided that, until they figured out who had gotten access to the back room, it might actually be safer in Sadie's shop than it would be at the library. She and Kimama had even considered moving all of the artifacts to Sadie's store, but there were so many of them that it would have been a production, and moving them actually posed risks as well. None of the other artifacts had even been touched, so there was a chance that whoever had damaged the instrument had been interested only in it and nothing else. So for the time being, Sadie was in possession of the instrument. She still thought she could likely repair it. But before she did, she wanted to get an expert opinion.

Dr. Gramas had been so fascinated by her description over the phone that he'd agreed to drive in that afternoon all the way from Denver, on what was little more than a moment's notice. Now he stopped in front of the instrument, which lay alone on the worktable, and took a deep breath.

"This is it?" he asked.

Sadie nodded. "As you can see, it's damaged," she said.

Dr. Gramas leaned down to peer at the long gap where the face of the instrument had separated from the back. "Yes," he said. "*Hmm*. Yes."

Then he straightened. "But it appears you were lucky. No splintering."

He gazed down on the intricate designs that decorated the face of the instrument. "And no visible damage to the design work. Which is…"

He peered closer again. "Remarkable," he finished.

His brow furrowed, but his eyes were bright with interest. "I don't know that I've ever seen anything like this," he said.

"That's what Kimama said," Sadie told him. She winked at him. "Of course, she's not a national expert. But she has seen quite a few of the artifacts in our community."

Dr. Gramas nodded, still staring at the designs.

"Do you know what tribe made it?" Theo asked.

"You say it's local?" Dr. Gramas asked. "From here in Colorado?"

"It's been in the hands of a local family for several generations," Sadie told him. "Other than that, we're not certain. The family was reluctant to put the instrument on display. And they haven't been terribly eager to share its history within the family."

That was a bit of an understatement, given her encounter with Beverly, but there was no reason to bring Dr. Gramas into all of that.

"Well," Dr. Gramas said, "there are several major groups of people here in Colorado."

"I thought the Ute tribe were the only people native to Colorado," Theo said.

Dr. Gramas smiled at him.

"You've got that part right," he said. "They've been here the longest. Their own history says they've been here since the beginning of time. But they didn't think of themselves as a unified tribe. Before European settlers arrived, they were distinct groups of nomads. They interacted closely with each other, but not under any one leader or system."

"But there's a Ute reservation in Colorado," Theo said.

"That's right," Dr. Gramas said.

"What is Ute culture like?" Sadie asked.

"Dance is a significant part of it," Dr. Gramas said. "They celebrate both a Bear Dance and a Sun Dance."

"So they probably have a lot of instruments," Sara commented.

Dr. Gramas nodded. "Yes," he said. "But most of them are percussive. The Bear Dance, historically, is accompanied by large drums and hand drums. And a Ute instrument that settlers described as a *morache*."

"What's a morache?" Sara asked.

"It's a rattle, made from a notched stick, with a resonator," Dr. Gramas said.

"Which is pretty different from this," Theo said, looking down at the instrument.

Dr. Gramas nodded.

"So what other native people live in Colorado?" Sara asked. "And if the Ute are the only people native to Colorado, how did they get here?"

"Well, there are also the Navajo, in the southwest," Dr. Gramas said. He pulled out a map from his bag and spread it on the table, pointing to the corner where Colorado, New Mexico, Arizona, and Utah met. At the corner, a large block of land that spread over Utah, New Mexico, and Arizona was marked "Navajo Nation."

Theo let out a low whistle. "That's a big piece of land," he said.

"It's the largest reservation in the United States," Dr. Gramas said. "Twenty-seven thousand square miles."

"And beautiful land," Alice commented.

Dr. Gramas nodded again. "Yes," he said. "Some of the most beautiful in the world."

"But it's not in Colorado," Sara said, pointing at the map. The borders of the reservation seemed as if they should naturally reach up into the corner of Colorado as well, but instead the boundary was cut off by a sharp right angle at the Colorado state lines.

"You've got a keen eye," Dr. Gramas said. "The reservation doesn't extend into Colorado. But that doesn't mean there weren't

Navajo people here. Or that they didn't influence Colorado culture. And, of course, there are still Navajo people in Colorado today."

"But they weren't the first people here," Sara asked. "Because the Ute were."

Dr. Gramas nodded.

"So where did the Navajo come from?" Theo asked.

"From western Canada," Dr. Gramas said. "Probably in the 1200s. There was a great civilization in the American West until then, the Anasazi. But that civilization collapsed around that time, and historians believe that the Navajo may have moved south in the aftermath.

"They were a nomadic people," Dr. Gramas went on. "Like the Ute. They didn't organize into a single political structure until the 1700s. But the Spanish identified them as distinct from other groups because of their command of agriculture."

"They were farmers?" Sara asked.

Dr. Gramas nodded. "Yes," he said. "And there's been a very interesting development in ancient Navajo history recently."

"What's that?" Sadie asked.

Dr. Gramas raised his eyebrows and sighed. "I have to admit, I was skeptical about it at first myself," he said.

"About what?" Alice asked.

"Well, for years, some people have been observing that Navajo culture seems similar to the culture of Tibet," Dr. Gramas said. "They have similar cosmologies, and creation myths, which was never all that convincing to me, because it's easy to find similarities in religious systems—just like it's easy to find differences."

"Sometimes too easy," Sadie said.

Dr. Gramas smiled wryly. "But some of the cultural overlap is genuinely striking," he went on. "Both cultures are famous for their love of turquoise. Both have a tradition of mandala sand paintings. And recently…"

Sadie glanced at Theo and Sara as Dr. Gramas paused for effect, and was pleased to see that both of her grandchildren seemed to be as transfixed by his history lesson as she was. They were both staring at him with rapt concentration, as if waiting to watch the last moments of a gripping movie.

"Yes?" Theo said, hardly able to bear the wait.

"They conducted genetic tests on both the Navajo and Tibetans," Dr. Gramas said.

"And?" Sara demanded.

"They're similar enough that some scientists now believe that they're related people groups," Dr. Gramas said. "There's enough evidence there to make a credible argument that the Navajo are descended from Tibetans who made their way from Asia to the Americas over the Bering Strait, and that they imported elements of their original culture more or less whole to the American continents."

"The Bering Strait," Sara said, calculating. "That's between Russia and Alaska."

Dr. Gramas nodded. "You've got it," he said.

"But that's a lot of water," Sara objected.

"It is," Dr. Gramas said. "About fifty miles. But the water's shallow."

"Shallow enough to believe that at one time it might have been land?" Theo asked.

"You've got it," Dr. Gramas repeated, to Theo this time.

"That's amazing to think of," Alice said. "This would have been well before the thirteenth century even."

"If the Bering Strait theory is true, people would have had to cross it before the land bridge was submerged," Dr. Gramas said. "And as far as historians can tell, it's been submerged for thousands of years."

"There's so much history we don't know," Alice said, with a tone of faint wonder.

Dr. Gramas nodded. "That's part of why I love to study it. I loved history, even when I was a kid. But it got taught to me as if it jumped straight from ancient Greece to the Wars of the Roses, with maybe a few skirmishes in the Far East. But there were giant empires in the Americas, and in Africa, that I learned very little about."

"Why not?" Theo asked.

"Part of it is because some of that history was passed through oral traditions, instead of written down," Dr. Gramas said. "And part of it has to do with the history between Europeans and these specific groups."

"Cowboys and Indians," Sara said.

"Well, it goes back a bit further than that," Dr. Gramas said. "But, yes. Because we were in conflict with these people, we weren't as interested in learning their history. In fact, sometimes we went out of our way to pretend they didn't have civilizations that mattered to the world. At least, not as much as ours did."

"Well, I love learning about native history," Theo said. "But I've got to say, it seems like Europeans have affected the world a lot more than Native Americans."

"You might not say that once you get to know the history better," Dr. Gramas said with a wink. "For instance, do you like pizza?"

"Of course!" Theo said.

"I like *real* Italian food," Sara said, with a provoking glance at her older brother. "Like spaghetti and lasagna."

"What you're really saying is that you like Native American food," Dr. Gramas said.

"What?" Theo yelped.

Sadie grinned. "I've heard this before," she said. "The tomato is from the Americas, isn't it?"

Dr. Gramas nodded. "That's right," he said. "Not Italy. And so is the potato," he went on, "which is a cornerstone of European wealth. It finally stabilized the food supply in Europe, so that people could stop cycles of starvation and begin to build life as we know it.

"And those aren't just examples of ingenious Europeans finding value in something Native Americans hadn't figured out how to use," he continued. "The potato, for instance, is poisonous in its natural state. Expert Peruvian farmers had spent generations domesticating them, and cultivating different varieties. It was when we took them back to Europe that we were too careless to take more than a few strains. That left the handful of varieties in Europe vulnerable to disease—and ultimately caused the Irish potato famine."

"I never knew all that," Sara said.

"But every teenager in Silver Peak will know by tomorrow," Sadie said, giving her granddaughter's hair a tender rumple.

"And it's not just agriculture," Dr. Gramas said. "Americans like to trace the history of democracy all the way back to the ancient Greeks. But there's actually a lot of evidence that it was contact with Native American civilizations that helped the founding fathers imagine a political system that was different from the one they left behind in Europe. The Iroquois Nation had a federal system that encompassed various states long before we did. Ben Franklin was calling for the United States to imitate that system in the 1750s, twenty years before the Declaration of Independence. And the ancient Greeks may have experimented with democracy, but they were hardly a beacon of democracy by the eighteenth century. So you can make a pretty interesting argument that it was actually Native Americans who gave the world modern democracy."

"I never heard that before," Theo said.

"And not every history teacher you have will agree with it," Dr. Gramas said. "But not all history teachers agree with each other about many other things either."

"You said there was another group of native people," Sadie said, bringing the conversation back around to the instrument again. "Here in Colorado. Who were they?"

"The Plains tribes," Dr. Gramas said.

"But Colorado is mountainous," Sara said. "Not made up of plains."

"Right again," Dr. Gramas said with a wink. "But as European settlers moved across the continent, a number of tribes were forced west. The Lakota, for instance, originally ranged from Wisconsin to the Dakotas. But population pressure forced them out on to the Great Plains. And along the way, some of them spent time in Colorado. So did the Comanche, and the Apache, and the Arapaho."

"So which of those tribes do you think might have had anything to do with this instrument?" Sadie asked. She loved history—that was why she spent her time living in the midst of it, among all the artifacts and treasures of her shop. And why she taught it before she retired. But no matter how great the story was, she never forgot to be practical. She always wanted to know what it had to do with the here and now. She didn't love history because she liked getting lost in the past. She loved it because it helped her understand the present.

Dr. Gramas picked up the instrument and turned it over in his hands, peering at the long neck, the taut strings, and the round belly. When he spoke next, Sadie let out a rush of breath. Until then, she hadn't even been aware that she was holding it.

"It's such an interesting piece," Dr. Gramas said.

"Which tribes made instruments like it?" Sadie asked.

"That's the thing," Dr. Gramas said. "It's not typical of any people from the area, even though so many lived and passed through Colorado. As I was telling Theo, the Utes, who have been in Colorado for the longest stretch of history, concentrated on percussive instruments. Other tribes might have had a broader array of instruments, but those typically included flutes, or instruments with one or two strings."

"This one has five," Sara observed.

"Yes," Dr. Gramas said. "Which makes it very unusual." He held the instrument by the neck and turned it this way and that, so that he could peer into the hole that lay just under the strings. "I just wish that—what's this?"

His voice jumped when he interrupted himself, and Sadie almost jumped along with him.

"What's what?" she asked quickly.

But Dr. Gramas had gone silent, peering even more intently into the shadowy belly of the instrument. "There are letters in here."

"Letters?" Theo asked. "But I thought native people didn't have an alphabet."

"They had systems of writing," Dr. Gramas said, still absorbed by whatever he could see inside the instrument. "But not an alphabet."

"What does it say?" Sara asked, trying to peek over Dr. Gramas's shoulder.

"Sara," Alice said, pulling her daughter back.

"I'm curious!" Sara complained.

"A...," Dr. Gramas read. "E..."

"They're letters from *our* alphabet?" Sara asked.

Dr. Gramas nodded and looked up. "AEBT," he said.

"What in the world does that mean?" Sadie asked.

7

_____

DR. GRAMAS SHOOK HIS HEAD. "I DON'T KNOW," HE SAID. "I'VE never seen anything like it."

He traced his finger over the patterns of native design that decorated the face of the instrument. "I can't read this either," he said. "But I've seen enough comparable designs to recognize that it's likely decorative. In other words, I don't believe it's primarily a message, although the images may convey some meaning. From other designs I've seen, these characters look like they're likely about family—a marital bond, protection for children."

"But then why would there be letters from the alphabet we use in English as well?" Sadie asked. "Is that unusual?"

"Of course, many native people learned European languages," Dr. Gramas said. "In order to trade. And to survive. You don't often see them side by side with traditional elements, as on this instrument. But it's not outside the realm of possibility."

"Well, in fact, I'd say it's firmly in the realm of reality," Sadie joked. "Since you're holding the instrument in your hands right now."

Dr. Gramas smiled. "That's right," he said.

"I just don't understand why the letters would be hidden," Sadie said.

"Maybe it's some kind of code," Theo said, with evident enthusiasm.

"Why would you write a code on the inside of a musical instrument?" Sara asked. "Why not just write it on a piece of paper?"

"It's easy to hand an instrument to another person," Theo said. *Although Sara's point was actually a good one,* Sadie thought. "It wouldn't arouse any suspicion."

"But how much information can you actually get across in four letters?" Sara asked.

"Maybe it's an anagram," Alice suggested. "AEBT could spell BEAT."

"That's a musical word!" Theo said triumphantly. "See?"

"See what?" Sara said. "What does it mean?"

"Are there any more letters in there?" Sadie asked. "Can you see anything at all?"

Dr. Gramas peered into the instrument again, shook his head, then handed it to her.

"Maybe you can see something I can't," he said.

Sadie peered into the shadows of the instrument as well. She could see the letters he had spied, clearly marked out in what looked to be red ink. As unfortunate as the damage was, it had probably made them easier to see. But just like him, she couldn't see anything else.

"It's so strange," she said. "Perhaps it's the signature of the person who made the instrument."

"Or the mark of the owner," Dr. Gramas suggested.

"And it'd be impossible to search for in a library or online," Sadie mused. "It's just a jumble of letters."

"It might mean something more to the family who's in possession of the instrument," Dr. Gramas said. "Have you asked them about it?"

Sadie's mind flashed back to the way Beverly's demeanor had changed when Kimama asked her for information about the instrument.

"I'm not sure why they even agreed to allow it to be a part of the exhibit, to be honest," Sadie said. "They haven't exactly been eager to share its history."

Dr. Gramas raised his eyebrows. "Well," he said, "remember, it's a family descended from settlers who somehow wound up with a native instrument. That hasn't always been a pretty history. So whatever it is, it might be something long-forgotten."

He paused, looking thoughtful. "Or something the family would very much like to forget."

Sadie laid the instrument back down on her worktable.

"What's your expert opinion on the repair?" she asked. "I feel confident that I can bring it back to the shape it was when it was lent to the library. And I know enough about archival practices to be confident that I can do that without compromising the integrity of the design or the materials. At least not any more than they've already been compromised. But it's such an unusual piece that I wanted to make sure you didn't have any reservations about my undertaking the work. Or that you see anything that I don't see."

"Well, what's your plan?" Dr. Gramas asked.

"To reattach the front to the body using archival glue and clamps," Sadie said.

"Bringing everything as close to flush as possible, or being guided by the existing wear lines, of course," Dr. Gramas added.

"Of course," Sadie said.

Theo glanced back and forth between his grandmother and Dr. Gramas, clearly taking notes in his own head. Sadie could see more clearly every day that Theo's goal to study to become a detective was a good choice.

Dr. Gramas laid his hand lightly on the belly of the instrument one final time. Then he looked at Sadie and grinned.

"Well, I'll tell you what," he said. "One of my good buddies is the head of restoration at the university in Denver. And I can't think of any way he'd do it differently."

"So you don't have any reservations?" Sadie asked.

"The only thing I'd have advised you to do is consult with a member of the people whose culture it came from," Dr. Gramas said. "And since I'm not able to help you establish that, I don't see how you'd be able to. And Kimama over at the library doesn't seem to have any more ideas than I do."

Sadie shook her head. "That's part of the reason she was so fascinated by this instrument," she said. "She's been curating exhibits of native artifacts for years. So she's got a very wide experience. But she wasn't able to place this."

"Well," Dr. Gramas said, "I'd say your next step is to repair it."

"And then what?" Sara demanded.

Dr. Gramas gathered his papers into his briefcase with a smile. "I'm not sure," he said. "But somehow I think your grandmother will come up with something." He grinned at Sadie.

"Thank you so much," Sadie said gratefully, as he picked up his briefcase.

"It's been a pleasure," Dr. Gramas said. "Like I said, I don't get to see a treasure like that every day. You'll let me know whatever you find out?"

8

As Dr. Gramas slipped out of the back room, his footsteps faded away toward the front of the shop, until the bell alerted them that the front door had been opened, and they vanished out into the street.

But then the bell over the door rang again.

"Did he forget something?" Sara wondered out loud.

Sadie headed into the shop, her family trailing behind her.

But when she stepped out onto the shop floor, it wasn't Dr. Gramas who stood just inside the door. It was Spike.

"Well, hello, Spike," Sadie said with a smile.

"Alice," Spike said, making it clear who he had really come to see.

Alice gave him a kind grin while Theo and Sara smirked at each other. It was easy for them to like Spike, because he and Alice's kids all had one thing in common: They were all fans of Alice.

And it was probably even easier for the kids to like him, Sadie reflected, because Alice so clearly wasn't interested in Spike. So he didn't pose any real threat to life as the kids knew it. He was just a pleasant surprise from time to time. And they got no end of amusement over his all-too-obvious crush on their mother.

"How are you doing?" Spike asked Alice, as the kids scattered around the shop to give them a chance to talk.

Sadie, however, stayed nearby. She had a few questions of her own she wanted to ask Spike.

"I'm fine," Alice said. "We were just meeting with an expert on native artifacts, to get his perspective on the instrument."

Spike's face fell at the mention of it. "From the library?" he said.

Alice nodded. Because of his evident distress, she seemed to feel the need to comfort him. "He says it's repairable," she told him.

Spike's eyes lit up. For the first time, he glanced at Sadie. "Completely?" he asked.

"Well," Sadie said, "I don't know if any repair is ever complete. We like to say in antiques that everything that happens to a piece leaves a mark, even if you can't see it. But I think I'll be able to get this pretty close to invisible."

"That would be wonderful," Spike breathed. "I can't tell you how terrible I feel about what happened."

"Well, it wasn't necessarily your fault," Alice said. "We still don't know what happened."

Sadie understood Alice's instinct to comfort her friend, but she wasn't ready to let Spike off the hook just yet. As much as the family liked Spike, and as unlikely as it sounded, until they knew what had happened to the instrument, they couldn't even be certain that he wasn't the one who had done the damage himself. And as much as Sadie hated to see him in distress, she still recognized that his nervousness about the instrument might, in fact, help her get some more information out of him.

"Actually," Sadie said, "I'm glad to see you. I'm curious about what exactly happened the night before the instrument got damaged."

Spike took a deep breath, looking as if he'd be happier talking about just about anything else in the world. But still, he collected the wherewithal to meet her eyes and nod. "Sure," he said. "Anything I can do."

"I remember you explained how you put the instrument in the case, checked the case, and then set it in the corner," Sadie said. "I'm just curious about a few of the details. Was there any kind of lock on the case?"

Spike shook his head.

"Nope," he said. "I remember Kimama mentioning that too. I think she would have felt a lot better if there was one. At the time, I thought she was a little overprotective. But now, I wish I had been more protective myself. But the case didn't come with a lock. It was an old one, and it hadn't been built with one. In fact," he added, "I don't think it was even built for the instrument."

"No?" Sadie asked, her eyebrows rising.

Spike shook his head.

"I mean, it's not a big deal. It happens all the time, especially with a handmade instrument. It can cost a lot for a handmade case. So people find a case for something else that just about fits, and they make it work. To me, this case looked like a case for a mandolin. I expect that's what it originally came with. And then maybe the mandolin got lost, or broken, and someone used it to protect this old native instrument instead."

"That's a very interesting story," Sadie said. "Is there any evidence of that?"

"I'm not sure I'd call it proof," Spike said, with a glance at Alice, who gave him an encouraging nod. "Maybe more like, just clues."

"Clues like what?" Sadie said.

"Do you have the instrument here?" Spike asked. "I can show you."

"Theo," Sadie called. "Do you mind watching the counter?"

Deeply absorbed in a stack of antique magazines, Theo raised his hand to let her know he'd heard and agreed.

Sadie led Spike back to the workroom. As they stepped in, he glanced over his shoulder to see if Alice had come with them, but she had politely slipped away.

Spike looked down at the broken instrument and grimaced.

"I still hate to see it this way," he said.

"It won't be this way for long," Sadie promised. "But can you show me what you mean, about the case?"

"Sure," Spike said, moving the instrument gently on the bright velvet. He showed Sadie a relatively large gap between the bottom of the instrument and the lower curve of the case. "See?" he asked.

Sadie nodded.

"That's not supposed to be there," Spike said. "It means the case is made for a bigger instrument. It's not the end of the world, because it fits real snug here, up where the neck fits in. But even there," he said, gingerly raising the instrument from the case. "You can see this isn't the first instrument that's been in this case."

"It isn't?" Sadie repeated.

"Nope," Spike said. "You see that?"

"What?" Sadie said.

Spike pointed to a pattern where the nap of the velvet had been pressed down over years by the neck of an instrument. Then he let the instrument in his hands settle back down into place, and pointed. "That," he said.

Now that he pointed it out, Sadie could see it clearly: The native instrument pressed into the same hollow, but not as deep. It didn't even touch the velvet for most of the length of the old impression. It must have been left by some other instrument.

"But it was this way when Kimama first let you play the instrument?" Sadie asked.

Spike nodded. "Yep," he said. "As soon as I took it out, I could see it didn't fit the case."

"But as far as the damage this week goes," Sadie said. "The case wasn't tampered with. Or replaced."

Spike let the empty case fall closed, and looked closely at the clasps.

"I wouldn't say so," he said. "It doesn't look like there was any damage done to the case at all, actually. Just the instrument."

"That's interesting," Sadie said. "It makes it seem as if someone *meant* to damage the instrument…"

"Why do you say that?" Spike asked, scratching his head.

"If it had been some kind of accident," Sadie explained, "I'd expect to see at least some kind of damage to the case. If someone dropped it by mistake, for instance. Or if they tripped over it. But the case isn't damaged. That probably means they took their time, and that they knew what they were doing."

"But why would someone go to all that trouble of being careful with the case, and then do"—Spike paused as he looked at the damaged instrument, which still clearly filled him with significant emotion—"*this* to the instrument?"

"I wish I knew," Sadie said, letting the two sides of the case fall back together, hiding the velvet inside.

She looked back up at Spike. "But let's move on through the last time you saw the instrument before it was damaged. You told us you put it back where Kimama had indicated."

Spike nodded vigorously. "Yep," he said. "Just like I had every night. And I'd been working with it for a couple of weeks. So I knew the drill. It wasn't like I was doing it for the first time."

"Did you notice anything strange about the back room?" Sadie asked. "Was there anything out of place?"

"Nope," Spike said. "It was just like any other day at the library. Kimama's real organized, so there was never anything else in that space. I just finished up, popped the instrument back into the case, and set it right in the corner, where it belonged."

"And that was quite late in the day, wasn't it?" Sadie asked.

Spike cracked a grin. "I think you and I might have pretty different ideas of what we mean by late," he said.

Sadie smiled back at him. "Oh, I don't know. You might be surprised," she joked back. Then her face turned serious. "What I meant was that you said you finished after the library closed," she said.

Spike nodded. "That's right," he said. "I heard her make the announcement that they'd be closing soon. That's when I started packing up."

"So the library was empty when you left?" Sadie asked.

"It was getting that way," Spike said. "Kimama runs a tight ship, but she does give people some time if they need to get their things together. Or if there's a mom who's just finishing up reading a book to a kid."

"So sometimes there would be people there for a few minutes after hours?" Sadie asked.

Spike nodded.

"What about the night before the instrument was damaged?" Sadie asked. "Do you remember anyone else around the place?"

9

Spike's brow furrowed in concentration. "I can't say I remember anyone specifically."

"But there were people there?" Sadie said.

Spike shrugged his shoulders, a helpless look on his face. "I wish I could say for sure," he said. "The problem is that I was in and out of there so often. It all kind of blends together. I remember seeing some people there as I was going out some nights. But I'm not sure if it was that night, or another one."

Sadie sighed.

"But I never saw anything out of the ordinary," Spike went on. "I mean, nobody was ever real interested in what I was doing. Or sneaking around, acting suspicious. As far as I could tell, it was pretty much always a bunch of parents, just trying to get their kids to get it together to get out the door once Kimama made the closing announcement."

Sadie wished that Spike was able to give her more detail, but what he was telling her was more than believable. She'd spent enough time in the library herself to know that what he was describing was true more times than not.

But still, even if everything had seemed just the way it always did, something different had definitely happened that night.

"What about when you left the room?" Sadie continued. "What was the security like for the artifacts? Did you lock it? Did anyone else have a key?"

Spike shook his head. "I never had a key," he said. "But I was careful about making sure it was locked before I left the building. So what I'd do is to pack everything up, and then go find Kimama and have her lock up the room for me."

"And that's what you did that night?" Sadie asked.

"Sure," Spike said. "Just like I did every night."

"And how long did it take you to find Kimama?"

Spike looked at her with surprise. "About as long as it took to walk from one end of the library to the other side."

"But while you did that, the room would have been unlocked," Sadie said.

"I guess so," Spike said. "But anyone in the library would have been able to see someone go in or out of it."

"If they were looking," Sadie said. In the rush of getting last-minute books checked out, and making sure that the library floor was empty of patrons, nobody might have been looking, she thought.

"Are you saying you think someone snuck in while my back was turned?" Spike asked.

"I'm not saying anything yet," Sadie said. "I'm just trying to understand a little bit better what exactly could have happened."

"Well, they would have had to have been pretty fast," Spike said. "I mean, it took me about a minute and a half to get from the back room to Kimama at the desk."

"Yes," Sadie said. "But then you had to get her attention. And she had to come back with you. Did you ever have to wait for her to finish working with a patron before she was able to come lock up the room?"

"I guess a few times," Spike said.

"What about the night the instrument was damaged?" Sadie asked.

Spike gave his head a decisive shake. "Nope," he said. "I actually remember, that went pretty fast. She had James checking out the last few customers, so when she saw me coming, she came right out from behind the counter, and we went back and she locked it up. She checked that it was locked, and then she had me check it. That was our little security measure."

Sadie was touched by the evident care both Spike and Kimama had tried to show in taking responsibility for the safety of the instrument. But that only made her more determined to understand who in the world would have tried to damage it.

"So that whole exchange took you what, perhaps two minutes?" she said.

"Two or three," Spike said. "I guess."

Sadie calculated what she knew about the plan of the library in her head. She would have loved to have ruled out the possibility of someone slipping into the back room while Spike's back was turned, but she couldn't. The library was spacious for a small town, but the floorplan was still condensed enough that a person could have made it to the back room, and slipped into it, from almost any part of the library, given that much time.

"That's enough time for someone to sneak in, isn't it?" Spike asked.

Sadie nodded. "But if someone was in there," she said, "then you and Kimama would have locked them in."

"Oh no," Spike said. "It wasn't built that way. Probably because they've got so many kids in the library. You can unlock it from inside, no problem."

"So if someone was hiding in there, after they damaged the instrument...," Sadie began.

"They could just have walked out," Spike finished for her.

"But how would they have gotten out of the library?" Sadie asked.

"Same way," Spike said. "That's part of how Kimama did the closing every night. She'd lock the doors so that new visitors couldn't come in. But anyone who was already inside could still get out."

Sadie sighed. "That's very interesting," she said.

"Do you think that's what happened?" Spike asked.

"I don't know," Sadie said. "But it's an interesting option."

"But who would want to do a thing like that?" Spike asked.

Sadie took a deep breath. "You say your friend Steven was with you in the back room earlier in the day," she said.

Spike raised his hands defensively. "I know you don't know him like I do, so I can't blame you for that. But he's a good man. He might be going through a hard time, but he wouldn't do a thing like that."

"I don't want you to think I'm accusing anyone," Sadie said. "But I'd just like to get some perspective on anything unusual that happened that day."

"It's not so unusual for Steven to come help me on a musical project," Spike said. "He and I have played together for years."

"But he hadn't visited you at the library before," Sadie said.

Spike shook his head. "No."

"Have you talked with him since the instrument was damaged?" Sadie asked.

"No," Spike said. "We usually would have had practice last night, but we didn't."

"Why not?" Sadie asked.

"Steven had something come up," Spike said.

As Sadie searched his face, he raised his hands again. "Don't ask me what it was," he said. "I don't know. I'm hoping it had something to do with a job. These days, he's been looking for anything, so whenever a possible job opening comes up, he's got to drop everything."

Sadie nodded, trying not to look too openly skeptical.

"I know what you're thinking," Spike said. "But it didn't have anything to do with the instrument. I don't want you to make up some whole story in your head. The bottom line that you should be taking from this is that Steven is a man who will do anything to take care of his family. Even when times are hard."

"Anything?" Sadie asked.

"He's not a thief, Sadie," Spike said. "Or a vandal."

"Still," Sadie said, "I think I'd like to talk with him. Maybe he saw something that you didn't while he was in the room, or in the library. Something that could help us. You said he's working part-time?"

"Yeah," Spike said, seeming somewhat mollified. "He helps out Carmella over at Bless Our Souls Jewelry in the shop most days. And when they haven't got anyone in the store, she lets him use the equipment in the back to work on his own jewelry line. Like I told you, he's a hard worker."

"He even found a way to work two jobs when he's only working part-time," Sadie said.

"That's right," Spike said with a smile. "He's a good guy."

In the front of the shop, the phone began to ring.

A moment later, Theo appeared in the door, holding out the portable handset. "Grandma," he said. "It's for you."

Sadie reached for the phone, mouthing, "Who?"

"Kimama," Theo whispered. "At the library."

"Kimama," Sadie said when she lifted the receiver to her ear. "How are you?"

"Fine, fine," Kimama told her, in a voice so tight with strain that Sadie knew immediately that she was anything but.

"What's going on?" Sadie asked.

"Could you come over to the library?" Kimama asked.

"Is everything all right?" Sadie said.

"I can show you when you get here," Kimama said. "Something else has happened."

10

SADIE BUSTLED UP THE FRONT STEPS OF THE LIBRARY SO FAST that she almost knocked into a pair of elementary-school girls who were on their way out, both struggling under the weight of large stacks of books.

One of them tripped trying to get out of Sadie's way, and a book toppled from her stack, but Sadie caught it before it hit the ground, and carefully replaced it in the girl's arms.

The girl, a tomboyish blonde with curious gray eyes, thanked her.

With an apologetic smile, Sadie stepped into the library.

James was manning the desk. He greeted her with a shy smile.

"How are you doing today?" Sadie asked.

"Oh," he said, "fine. Are you here to see Kimama?"

Sadie nodded.

"She's in the back," he said, pointing to the room where just a few days before they'd discovered the damaged instrument. "With the sheriff."

"Thanks so much," Sadie said, heading over. *The sheriff?* she wondered. What in the world had happened that required more police involvement in the once-quiet library?

As she threaded her way through the shelves of books to the back, Sadie felt the quiet tug at her heart that sometimes let her know that it would be good to pray. *Lord,* she said, *I don't know what I'm walking into. But You do...Please show me where You are, whatever I find.*

At the door to the back room, she paused and knocked.

Kimama opened the door. She was obviously making an effort to keep herself under control. But she was just as obviously deeply upset.

Beside her stood Sheriff Mac Slattery. He gave Sadie a friendly nod, but it was clear that his mind was preoccupied with something as well.

"Thank you for coming," Kimama said, stepping back to let Sadie in the room.

From the expression on her face, Sadie had been afraid that some kind of major damage might have been done to the storage room. But that wasn't the case. Everything still seemed to be in its proper place, neatly arranged, just as it had been before.

"What's going on?" Sadie asked.

Kimama pushed her hair back. "Something strange," she said. "I came in this morning, and nothing was where it belonged."

Sadie looked around at the organized stacks of boxes.

"Have you spent all morning cleaning up?" she asked.

Kimama shook her head. "No," she said. "This is what it looked like when I arrived. I left it just the way it was, because I wanted the sheriff to see it too."

Sadie's eyebrows drew together. "What do you mean?"

"I know," Kimama says. "It all looks fine, right?"

"Almost as if it'd been organized by a librarian," Sadie joked, to add a little lightness to the situation.

"But apparently it's not organized the right way," Sheriff Slattery said, his expression still puzzled.

"Nothing is where it belongs," Kimama added, in something like a tone of wonder. "The whole place has been rearranged."

Sadie touched the box on the top of a stack that stood next to her, just inside the door.

"Like that one," Kimama said. "That belongs in the opposite corner."

"What do you mean, 'belongs'?" Sheriff Slattery asked.

"I had a whole system," Kimama said. "It's how I kept track of where all the artifacts were while we were staging them to put up for the exhibit."

"Does your system have a catalog?" Sadie asked. "Or is it all in your own head?"

"It's mostly up here," Kimama said, tapping her temple. "But there is a logic to it. They were arranged more or less according to where they would appear in the display cases outside."

"Did anyone know this besides you?" Sheriff Slattery asked.

Kimama nodded. "Sure," she said. "Anyone who helped me install the exhibit would have gotten a general sense of it. The library staff. Probably half a dozen other volunteers."

"You say they were in order according to their location in the display out in the library," Sadie said. "But now...?"

Kimama looked around. "It's totally random," she said. "I have no idea why anyone would do anything like this."

"Is anything broken?" Sheriff Slattery asked.

Kimama nodded. "That's the first thing I thought," she said. "But the reality is that the instrument that got broken was the only artifact we still had back here. Everything else had been put out on display when the exhibit went up, last week. I had been keeping back the instrument for the opening reception. Spike was going to play it, and then we were going to put it on display in a special spot in the case. I had the spot all labeled, to build up some excitement about it. But everything else had already been put out."

"So these are just...empty boxes?" Sheriff Slattery asked, his expression becoming even more bewildered.

Kimama nodded.

"And they were in a completely different order last night, when I locked the place up," she said.

"Is there any chance that someone was in the room when you locked the door?" Sadie asked, remembering her conversation with Spike.

Kimama shook her head. "Not unless they were hiding *in* a box," she said.

With that, the three of them surveyed the room.

"Actually," Sadie said, looking at some of the larger containers that had been used to ship or deliver the more substantial pieces, "that wouldn't be impossible."

"I guess not," Kimama said. "But why in the world would anyone go to all that trouble, just to move the boxes around?"

"There's nothing valuable left in any of these boxes?" Sheriff Slattery reconfirmed.

"That's what I spent the whole morning checking," Kimama said. "Going through them all again. If there's something there, I didn't find it."

"Kimama," Sheriff Slattery said, "you know I take this very seriously. And we still have an active investigation open on the damage to the instrument. But I'm afraid there's not much I can do here. I've been trying to think of what crime has been committed, and I can't come up with anything more than trespassing."

Kimama nodded. "I understand," she said. "But I just wanted you to see it with your own eyes. In case something else happens."

The radio at Sheriff Slattery's hip crackled.

"I'm sorry," he said. "I've got thorough notes on this. I need to get going now. Just call me if anything else happens."

"I will," Kimama promised, as he left the back room.

As the door thudded shut behind him, Sadie looked down at the box beside her. The address label that had been attached to it had peeled up slightly, revealing another address label beneath: the whole history of where the box had been before it arrived here. If only all antiques came with a history like that, where you could just peel back one layer to reveal the next, neatly labeled underneath it, Sadie thought.

"Maybe they weren't looking for something in the box," she said. "Maybe they were looking for something *on* the box."

"Information?" Kimama said. "An address?"

"Your guess is as good as mine," Sadie said. "How many boxes are there here? How many objects do you have in the exhibit?"

"Almost a hundred," Kimama said. She dropped her hands to her sides in a gesture of defeat. "So even if they were hunting for some kind of information, I don't have any idea where to start. And I can't understand what any of this has to do with the Granby instrument."

"If it even does," Sadie said.

Kimama glanced at her. "You don't think it does?" she said. "Do you think two separate people would break into this room, in a matter of days? When we've never had a break-in at the library before?" she added.

"I don't think anything one way or the other yet," Sadie said. "I just think it's good for us to keep in mind how much we don't know, until we're able to get some answers we can be sure of."

"But how are we going to do that?" Kimama asked. Her hand fell on an empty box with a hollow thud.

"May I take a look at the exhibit?" Sadie asked.

"Sure," Kimama said, in a tone that suggested she didn't understand what Sadie was thinking, but she was willing to try anything.

Leaving the back room, Kimama led Sadie through the library to the large state-of-the-art glassed-in exhibit cabinets that spanned much of the back wall and reached high overhead, taller than even a tall man.

They were filled with fascinating items: cooking implements, items of clothing, toys, figurines, drawings, hats and headdresses, and several beautiful outfits of regalia. Each was accompanied by a beautifully designed sign that explained their origin and meaning and their part in the history of their people, and also the object's connection with the people of the town of Silver Peak.

"You've done a beautiful job here," Sadie said.

Kimama drew a sharp breath. "It doesn't feel like it," she said.

"Some days it doesn't," Sadie says. "But that doesn't mean you haven't done something amazing."

"Thanks," Kimama said.

"And we're even going to get *this* space filled," Sadie said, pointing to the empty place that Kimama had reserved for the instrument. Beside it was the largest sign, explaining how rare the instrument was, describing its connection to the Granby family, and inviting one and all to come out for the official exhibit party, which would feature an appearance by the one and only Spike Harris, playing a new composition on the historic instrument.

"You think?" Kimama said.

"If I have anything to say about it," Sadie said. "I met with Dr. Gramas from Denver this morning. He agrees with me that the instrument can be repaired. I'm going to begin work on it immediately. It'll take some time to do it correctly, and then to let it set, but I don't see any reason why Spike shouldn't have it in his hands in plenty of time for the party."

Kimama smiled, but then her face twisted with worry. "That's great news," she said. "But until we know who's been in the library, moving things around—and breaking them—I don't feel like any of these things are safe."

She stared at the empty space where the instrument was meant to sit. "That reminds me," she said.

"Of what?" Sadie asked.

"You'd been wondering whether anything strange happened the day the instrument was broken," Kimama said.

Sadie nodded.

"Well, nothing in particular happened that day," Kimama went on. "But as soon as the exhibit went up, a few days earlier, we did have a person in here who seemed...strange."

"What kind of person?" Sadie asked.

"A man," Kimama said. "Middle-aged. Kind of quiet. But he spent a lot of time looking at the exhibit."

"That sounds like a compliment to your work," Sadie said. "What did you think was strange about it?"

"Just something about his way," Kimama said. "He didn't seem like a regular visitor. He was intense in his interest in the objects. And I remember thinking it was strange that he spent so much time looking at the empty space where the instrument was meant to be placed. James saw it too, actually. He said it was almost as if that man could see something there that the rest of us couldn't."

"That does sound strange," Sadie said.

"It was. He actually spent so much time with the exhibit that I went over and tried to engage him in conversation," Kimama said. "But he didn't seem to want to talk much. I couldn't get him to give me more than a yes or no answer. So I finally gave up and just let him be."

"So you didn't learn anything about him?" Sadie asked.

"Nothing," Kimama said. "And you know how unusual that is in a small town. Usually the problem is learning too much about your neighbor's business, not too little."

Sadie laughed and nodded in agreement.

"I didn't give it much thought at first," Kimama went on. "We do get all kinds of people through here. And if I've learned anything in my time as a librarian, it's that different people have very, very different reactions to the same things. And when the excitement with the broken instrument happened, it completely fled my mind. So I didn't think much of it—except that he came in again."

"Again?" Sadie said.

"Today," Kimama added.

"Oh?" Sadie asked.

"It was almost the same as before," Kimama said. "But this time, I was rattled by what had just happened in the back room.

I don't know whether this was fair to him, but I went right up to him again. I told him I had noticed how interested he'd been in the exhibit earlier this week, and asked him where he came from. He wouldn't give me a straight answer to that."

"So what did he tell you?" Sadie asked.

"Nothing!" Kimama said. "He just mumbled something about needing to go, and headed for the door."

"Are you talking about that man who was in this morning?" James asked. As they'd been talking, he'd come up from the desk, holding a sheaf of papers in his hands.

"Yes," Kimama said. "You saw him too?"

James nodded. "I'm sorry to interrupt," he said. "I just was hoping you could check over a few of these interlibrary loan forms for me."

"Of course," Kimama said. "I'll be just a minute."

"James," Sadie said, as he turned to go. "Did you get a chance to talk with the man who was in here?"

"Not really. I mean, I tried, but..."

"He didn't tell you much," Kimama finished for him.

James shook his head. "Just his name."

Both Kimama and Sadie looked at James with renewed interest.

"His *name?*" Kimama repeated. "That's a whole lot more than he told me. How in the world did you drag that out of him?"

"Oh," James said, "I mean, it was just his last name. I guess I didn't give him much choice. I just asked him if I could help him, you know: 'Is there anything I can do for you, Mr. ...'"

"And he gave you his name," Kimama said, her astonishment mixed with amusement.

James nodded.

"What was it?" Sadie asked.

James opened his mouth to speak. Then he went silent, his brows suddenly furrowed. For a long, sickening second, Sadie wondered if he'd forgotten the name. From the look on James's face, he seemed to be wondering the same thing.

Then his face brightened. "Kilgore," he said. "It was Kilgore. I remembered it because it was kind of a horror show name."

"Yes," Kimama agreed. "Not the kind of name where you have to guess about its original meaning."

"Did he tell you anything else at all?" Sadie asked.

James shook his head. "He just told me his name," he said. "And then he said he didn't need any help."

"Well, that helps us," Sadie says.

Kimama tilted her head to one side, ambivalent. "You think?" she said. "There must be a lot of Mr. Kilgores in the world."

"True," Sadie said. "But you said you both got a good look at him, right?"

Kimama and James both nodded.

Sadie headed to a nearby bank of computers, plopped down at one, and fired up the Internet search engine. "Well," she said, "then maybe you'll be able to recognize him if you see him again."

Quickly, she typed in the name *Kilgore*, and *Silver Peak*, then tried an image search. A group of images of Kilgore Creek, some government-related, some amateur, flashed up on the screen.

"I don't think that's him," James joked quietly.

"That was only our first try," Sadie acknowledged, already typing again.

This time, she tried *Mr. Kilgore*, and the name of the county that Silver Peak was situated in. This time, they discovered that their county was home to a perky dachshund who had apparently won a number of not just local but national dog shows. Although his given name was Benny, his owner's surname was Kilgore, and he apparently had a small legion of fans who called him by the pet name of "Mr. Kilgore."

"See what happens if you try searching *Kilgore* and *native*," Kimama suggested.

This time they had a bit better luck. Apparently there was a popular powwow in a town called Kilgore, which had been documented in thousands of pictures of beautiful regalia and ceremonial dances. But the town was in South Dakota, and although Sadie flipped quickly through the first dozen or so pictures, neither Kimama or James recognized anyone.

"Try *Kilgore, Colorado*," James said.

This brought up a suite of pictures of several Kilgore family clans. But after sifting through pictures of family dinners, anniversary portraits, and Little League games, Sadie's shoulders slumped.

She glanced up at Kimama. "I guess it's not as easy as I was hoping it might be," she said.

"Well, it's a tall order," Kimama said. "Finding someone with nothing but a last name and a face. Even for a librarian."

Sadie pushed back her chair and stood.

But as she did, James hurried to take her chair. Before he sat down, he glanced at Kimama. "I'd like to keep searching myself for a little while," he said. "If that's okay."

Kimama smiled. "This is actually a great test for a budding librarian," she said. "I feel like maybe I should write and recommend it to our licensing branch, as a potential final exam."

"I don't know if I'll find anything," James said. "I just don't want to give up yet."

"Well, it's fine with me," Kimama said. "As long as you understand that the assignment isn't complete until you relay any findings to your boss."

James grinned and tapped another query into the search engine. "You'll be the first to know," he said.

11

Sadie prayed for wisdom as she got out of her car on the curb outside the little bungalow that Beverly had been so insistent she and Kimama leave the day earlier.

She closed the car door gently behind her, and stepped across the escarpment onto the narrow lane of sidewalk that ran through Silver Peak's beautiful Victorian historic district. Then she took a deep breath, squared her shoulders, went up the walk to the familiar red door, and knocked.

A few seconds later, the door swung open, and Beverly stood there, framed by it.

Sadie opened her mouth, ready to make her case to ask Beverly to give her just a few more minutes of her time, instead of shutting her out again.

But to Sadie's surprise, Beverly's face split into a grin. "Sadie," she said. "I'm so glad you're here."

Sadie narrowly avoided blurting out, "You are?" Instead, she tried to return Beverly's warm smile. "Thank you so much for saying that," she said. "I was feeling bad about the last time we talked. I…"

"You know what," Beverly said, reaching out to pull Sadie inside, and guiding her into the same pretty sitting room where they had sat before, "I did too. That's why I'm glad you came. I hate that I might have given you the impression that I was upset about the instrument."

"Well," Sadie said, "I can understand why you would have been. It's a very rare piece. And it's been part of your own family's history."

Beverly's eyes seemed to flicker a bit as Sadie said this, but her smile didn't fade.

Relieved, Sadie went on. "Nobody in town may feel just the same way your family does about that instrument. But of anyone in town, I can promise you, Kimama cares the most about it."

"Oh, I could see that," Beverly said, waving her hand as the two of them sat down. "And I felt terrible that I made her feel any worse. I know it can't have been her fault. In fact, I'm almost glad she wasn't there when somebody did that damage. I have the feeling Kimama would have done just about anything to stop it. And I wouldn't have wanted her getting hurt herself."

Sadie tilted her head. "I hadn't thought of that," she said. "But you're right about one thing. Kimama would certainly have gone to great lengths to protect that instrument."

"So," Beverly said, "what brings you here today?"

Sadie shifted in her seat. "Well," she said, "I wanted to let you know our progress in repairing the instrument. I met with an expert from Denver earlier this morning. He thinks we'll be able to repair it to the point that the damage will be basically invisible to the naked eye. And it will still be playable."

Beverly beamed. "Well, that's wonderful," she said. "I'm so glad to hear it."

Sadie nodded. "I'm going to do the repairs myself. I've done some work like it before, and on some pieces of similar quality."

"You'd be my first pick," Beverly said. "Even if we had a room full of national experts. I'm sure you've got just as much skill as they do. And none of them would give it the care you'll give, because you know it's a hometown treasure."

"Thanks for the vote of confidence," Sadie said. "I'm going to do my best."

"I'm sure you will," Beverly said.

"I did talk with our expert from Denver a bit about the possible history of the instrument, as well," Sadie said.

"Oh?" Beverly said. Her smile was still friendly, but Sadie could see that it was also guarded, and she didn't prompt Sadie to go on by asking any follow-up questions.

Sadie pressed ahead anyway. Maybe, she thought, if she kept talking about the general history of the instrument, Beverly would be encouraged to share something she knew about the family's history with it. And however small, maybe that information would help her and Kimama to understand the strange events that had been going on at the library.

"It was an interesting conversation," Sadie said, and she paused again, hoping to pique Beverly's interest. But Beverly just looked at her, her unchanging smile growing stiff.

"He gave us a very interesting overview of the different people who have lived in Colorado throughout its history," Sadie said. "But he wasn't able to match the instrument with any of them. Apparently most of the native people in this area made music with drums. Or flutes or other percussion instruments. Stringed instruments weren't as common. And they usually had fewer strings than the instrument that's been in your family's hands."

Beverly nodded politely, but Sadie still got the sense that she couldn't wait for this conversation to be over.

"And there was something else interesting about the instrument," Sadie said. "Actually, the expert didn't point this out, but Spike did. He's the musician who was practicing on the instrument before it got damaged. He noticed that the instrument doesn't seem to fit the case. It's as if the case once held a completely different instrument. Probably one that was a bit larger."

Beverly gave a strained nod, clearly maintaining her civility with great effort. Sadie hated the idea of getting in another conflict with her. But she could also see that Beverly had to know something she wasn't telling. And with the whole exhibit at the library now under threat, perhaps from the mysterious visitor who might have damaged the instrument in the first place, Sadie wasn't willing to let politeness keep her from seeking out the truth.

"Do you know anything about that?" Sadie asked. "Did you ever hear anything about the case for the instrument, and how they came to be matched together?"

Beverly shook her head. "I can't say I have," she said. "In fact, I wouldn't have even remembered the instrument had a case if you hadn't mentioned it. Candace must have dug it up when she decided to give it to Kimama. And I didn't hear about any of that until after the fact."

"Oh!" Sadie said, surprised that Candace hadn't shared the decision to put the instrument on display with her mother. "I'm surprised she didn't tell you. You two seem so close."

"Well, you know," Beverly said. "I'm sure she didn't think it was much of a big deal."

Sadie's mind flashed back to Kimama's stories of all the years she'd spent making unsuccessful requests for the Granby family to share the instrument with the Silver Peak community at the library exhibit. Clearly, they hadn't thought it was no big deal to lend the instrument out during all that time. But Sadie decided to hold her tongue about that—at least for the time being. She didn't want to get in an argument. She just wanted to elicit as much information as she could.

Mentioning the case had been a warm-up for Sadie. What she was really interested in was Beverly's reactions to the mysterious letters on the inside of the instrument. Now she eased into that topic.

"We did find something else interesting when we looked closely at the instrument, though," Sadie said.

Beverly's smile had faded to a straight line. "Oh?" she said.

Sadie nodded. "I'm sure you're familiar with the beautiful native designs on the face of it. But did anyone in your family ever notice that there are English letters, as well?"

For the first time, Beverly seemed to have some real interest in the story. But her interest took the form of alarm. "There are?" she asked, the surprise in her voice evident.

"Yes," Sadie told her. "They're not easy to see, at least, ironically, not until the instrument was damaged. But that's what we bring the experts in for." She smiled. "They're actually on the inside of the instrument."

"What do they say?" Beverly demanded.

"It's just a set of letters," Sadie said. "They don't seem to mean anything, at least not immediately. They seem more like a signature, or perhaps a monogram. Except that there are four letters, instead of three. The expert thought that perhaps someone in your family might know something about them. Or that they might mean something to you if you heard them."

Beverly was watching Sadie closely now. She seemed as if she could barely wait to hear what she had to say next.

"AEBT," Sadie said. "Those are the letters. Do they mean anything to you?"

Beverly deflated with a whoosh of breath. But when she did, her face composed itself into the lines Sadie had seen earlier: friendly, but still distant. "No," she said, trying to keep a light tone. "I can't say that they do."

"The expert also said that anything the family could share with him about the instrument might help him connect it to a specific group of people," Sadie said. "I know you said you don't know much about the history, but if you remember anything at all, it might also help Kimama with the exhibit. Sometimes people don't think they know much about an old object, especially if it's been in the family for years. But if you can remember anything you've ever heard about it, however small, it could be a great help."

"I don't," Beverly said, shortly.

"It seems like the kind of thing kids would be curious about," Sadie said. "Even if you yourself were interested in other things when you were young, did you ever hear your brothers and sisters ask about it? Or your cousins?"

Beverly gave her head a quick shake. "Nope," she said.

Sadie was starting to worry that she might be pushing Beverly to the same point she'd been at on their earlier visit, when these kinds of questions had brought the conversation to such an unpleasant end. So she decided to back off into a broader range of questioning.

"Now, I know your family has been in Silver Peak for years," Sadie said with a smile.

At this, Beverly seemed to relax again. She even leaned forward, and gave what Sadie thought might be her first real smile of the visit. "That's right," she said. "Generations."

"When did the first Granbys come to Silver Peak?" Sadie asked.

"You know," Beverly said, "it's hard to say. Because both my mother's and my father's family have been here for so long. My great-grandfather built the very first mill in town," she said proudly. "Everyone was used to working with those wide, lazy rivers out East. They said he'd never be able to get something working on one of our wild Colorado creeks. But he showed them. With his own design, actually. He'd studied engineering before he came out here. And he was able to create a wheel that was smaller, so it wasn't as vulnerable to the force of rushing water. But it turned more quickly, because of the power of the water. And it turned out, it was even more effective than most mills operating in the East at that time."

"So he's one of the people who built this whole community," Sadie said.

Beverly nodded. Her pride in her family was evident. And it gave Sadie a hint as to why she might be so passionate about not sharing the story of the instrument. She obviously put so much stock in her respect for her family that it might be very hard for her to think about any events that didn't fit in with the family stories she liked to believe.

"That's right," Beverly said. "And then his son, my grandfather, put his building skills to work actually building the community. He was one of the original contractors in town. If you go back into the town records, you'll find his name on a lot of the permits, especially in this historic part of town. In fact, he was the builder even before they had permits. It's a little hobby of mine, researching the addresses he worked on. And I found a trove of his business papers a few years ago that let me know about dozens I hadn't known about before, because they were built before the city records were registering the names. In fact, what I discovered was that he was the builder who helped build the original city office."

Her eyes sparkled with the delight of the discovery. Sadie knew that same feeling well—it was what drew her to the work she did with antiques in her own store. But as she recognized the kindred spirit in Beverly, she became even more curious about the history Beverly was hiding. If Beverly had gone to all these lengths to discover the history of her grandfather, and her great-grandfather, it was hard to believe that she'd never shown any curiosity about the unusual instrument that had been in her family's possession for so long.

"What about those initials we found in the instrument?" Sadie tried. "AEBT. Did you ever see anything that might have had to do with them in the papers you researched? I wonder if perhaps it came into your family through a trade. At the mill? Or through the building company?"

Beverly's smile became tight again. "No," she said. "I never did. And anything relating to the instrument wouldn't have been found in the papers from that side of the family. It came through my mother's side."

"So your mother's people must have been in the area for some time, as well," Sadie said. "You're Silver Peak, through and through."

Beverly clearly took this as a compliment. Her elusive smile returned again. "That's true," she said. "My mother's people have actually been here even longer than my father's. They were some of the very first pioneers to come through these mountains, before Colorado was even a state. Their original place isn't even in town—it's out in the pines. My great-grandfather on that side had the idea that he'd left the city behind in Chicago. So he wasn't real keen about building another one. To him, he was a rich man if he just had a bit of land big enough that he didn't have to wake up every morning and see the next man waking up on his."

"He sounds like a real pioneer," Sadie said.

Beverly nodded. "We still have that property," she said. "It's rough. No plumbing at all, just an outhouse and a pump. And apparently the kids didn't much take to the rustic conditions. And they were real smart. Their dad might not have cared much about material things, but his son sure did. Just as soon as he was old enough, he started his own little patch of the garden, and began selling vegetables around to the other members of the settlement. His vegetable basket grew into a vegetable cart. And before he was twenty, he had opened the first grocery in Silver Peak."

"That's fascinating," Sadie said.

"Oh, I don't know why it would be fascinating to anyone outside of our family, really," Beverly said, somewhat bashfully.

"But it's not just the history of your family," Sadie said. "It's the history of this whole town. That's one of the things I always think is so interesting when I get the chance to research antiques. A lot of people think like you do, that it's just a piece of old family junk.

But that's almost never the case. These stories shed light on how life is for all of us now. Who knows? If your ancestors had never created that mill, or the grocery, or built the houses they did, Silver Peak might never have been strong enough to survive as a community. Plenty of pioneers came out and tried to put down roots in places that aren't even on the map anymore."

"Ghost towns," Beverly said.

Sadie nodded. "Exactly," she said. "And it sounds to me like that's what your family helped keep Silver Peak from becoming. So everyone who's enjoyed life here for all of these years owes something to them."

As she said it, though, she thought of the stories Dr. Gramas had just told her that morning, of all the people who had been here before Beverly's family arrived. The early pioneers hadn't just been painting on a blank canvas. There had been whole civilizations in place when they came to the land that was now known as Silver Peak.

The stories Sadie and Beverly knew about their own families were true. Their ancestors had taken big risks to build new communities in what seemed like wilderness to them. They'd worked hard to chase a dream, and to protect and provide for their families. They'd suffered along the way. And they'd built something special. Sadie loved Silver Peak just as much as Beverly did. She couldn't imagine life without it.

But still, she wondered how the story might look from the point of view of the people who had already been there when Beverly's family first arrived. To Beverly and Sadie, their family history looked like a story of risk, and struggle, and triumph. But how would it look from the point of view of the people who had made the instrument?

12

As she wondered this, Sadie's eyes moved around the room, taking in the decorations that were scattered on the tables and shelves between the pretty chintz furniture. Then her gaze caught on something. It was a picture of Beverly, giving a big smile alongside a woman who was obviously quite a bit older than she was. And the picture was recent—Sadie recognized it as being from the previous summer by the distinctive decorations that they'd put up the previous year at the Silver Peak Summer Festival. The new theme of the festival had been a huge topic of controversy. The year before, it had been undersea adventure. And Sadie could clearly see the face of a cardboard cutout of a diver in an old-fashioned diving uniform in the back of the picture.

"Is this a relative of yours?" Sadie asked, nodding at the picture, her heart quickening at the idea of getting to talk with someone in an earlier generation about the instrument.

Beverly smiled. "That's my mother," she said, with a laugh. "Although you wouldn't know it from the way she gets around town these days. She went into the nursing home after my dad passed away, several years ago. I was worried at first about how that would be for her. I didn't want her to feel like that meant she had officially gotten old. But I swear, I think she gets out more now than I do."

"They do have so many great programs over there at the home," Sadie agreed.

Beverly raised her hands in agreement. "I know!" she said. "She's out with a group this afternoon doing volunteer gardening, helping get the yards in order for people who aren't able to do it themselves for one reason or another. A few nights ago she was taking a salsa lesson, if you can imagine. It was just an introductory lark, she told me, but when I talked to her the next morning she said she was going to try to make a habit of it. Apparently she finds the instructor dashing."

"That's wonderful," Sadie said. "It's always so great to see people really living life, at every age."

"It definitely gives me something to live up to," Beverly said. "It was hard for me when my own husband passed away. It felt like he was so young. We should have had more time together. It'd be easy to just retreat into my home and think my life was over. But then I see what my mother is doing, twenty years older than me. And that doesn't leave me with much of an excuse."

"It sounds to me like she's still setting a great example for you," Sadie said. "And I always thought that was about the best thing parents could do for their children."

Beverly smiled. Her expression was so warm and open that it gave Sadie the courage to ask her next question.

"I would love to get her perspective on the instrument," Sadie said.

This time, Beverly's smile didn't just grow tight. It vanished completely, replaced by an expression of fear, and defensiveness, as if Sadie had somehow just tried to threaten something that was very precious to her.

"It would just be wonderful to get the perspective of someone from an earlier generation," Sadie went on, hoping she might be able to take the edge off of whatever Beverly was afraid of by reminding her that she was only trying to help with the family history that Beverly clearly cared about so much. "It's so easy for a family story to get lost down through the ages. But your mother would have lived closer to the time when the instrument came into the family. She might even have known the person who first came into possession of it. Or at least heard a story or two about it. And as the expert was saying today, any small thing that she remembers would help us."

But as Sadie went on, Beverly's expression didn't soften. Instead, her eyes grew even more distant.

"It could be a fascinating story, whatever connection your family had with native people," Sadie said. "It seems like there must have been some kind of relationship between them, for them to give your family the instrument."

Of course, Sadie thought, *not everything that settlers got from native people was freely given.* Much of it was taken by force. Perhaps Beverly knew more about that than she was willing to admit. Or perhaps she just knew enough about the difficult history to know that she didn't want to know any more than she did.

In any case, for her, the conversation was clearly over once more.

"I'm sorry," Beverly said. "I know that this exhibit at the library is important to Kimama. But to be honest, if Candace had asked me in advance, I can't say that I would have given my consent to put the instrument on display. I love learning my family history, but I don't feel a need to show it off to the whole community. And as I've been saying, we simply don't know much about the instrument."

But by the way her eyes slid to the side as she said this, Sadie could tell again that she wasn't being entirely truthful.

"Well," Sadie said, trying to keep the tone light, "maybe I could have a short conversation with your mother about anything she might remember. It's no problem for me to spend the time. And if she can't remember anything at all, maybe I could at least get a salsa lesson out of it."

Beverly didn't even make a polite attempt to laugh at Sadie's joke. Instead, her expression grew even more intense. "I think we've talked about this instrument enough," she said. "I wouldn't like to continue these conversations. And I think it would be a very bad idea to bother my mother about this."

"I see," Sadie said, rising from her seat. "Thank you so much for sitting with me. I'm going to do everything I can to restore the instrument."

"I mean it," Beverly said, as she steered Sadie to the door. "Do not speak with my mother about this."

"Thank you again," Sadie said as she stepped through the door Beverly had opened, feeling increasingly awkward about the tone the conversation had taken, but still trying to keep her own voice polite and friendly.

Then the red door swung shut behind her, and she found herself heading down the walk to her car once again.

But now she had even more questions than she'd had when she arrived, looking for answers. She'd thought at first that Beverly was just uncomfortable with the topic of the instrument for some reason, and that perhaps she could be persuaded to talk. But what she'd discovered was a resistance to talking about the instrument that was even fiercer than she could have originally guessed.

And it didn't just seem to have to do with Beverly protecting her own rosy image of her family, as Sadie had first assumed. Instead, she seemed to have the most emotion about making sure that her mother wasn't involved in conversations about the instrument in any way. She had so much emotion that Sadie wondered to what lengths she would go to shield her mother from the topic of the instrument.

Clearly, Beverly had never meant for the instrument to go on display. But if it did, Sadie certainly wouldn't be the only person in town who would think the topic was of interest. And that meant that she wouldn't be the only person in town who might start asking questions of Beverly's mother, especially if she was as involved in town activities as Beverly said.

Beverly obviously felt incredibly strongly about protecting her mother. So what kind of lengths would Beverly have been willing to go to, to keep the instrument from going on display?

Could she have even gone so far as to have done the damage herself, thinking that it might keep the instrument out of the public eye permanently?

But what could drive her to do such a thing?

What kind of secret was she trying to keep?

13

"THANKS SO MUCH FOR COMING WITH ME," SADIE SAID, AS SHE and Roz walked up the street from the Antique Mine to the Bless Our Souls jewelry store, where Spike said his friend Steven had been working.

"You don't need to ask me twice," Roz said. As evidence, she lifted her wrists, which as usual were decorated with a vast array of bangles. Today she seemed to have indulged a penchant for copper and turquoise. There was a thick copper cuff, decorated with a large turquoise stone, and a set of thin copper bangles, each printed with a slightly different native pattern. And then there was a separate set of bangles, which Roz had split, some on to one wrist, and some on to the other. These were also copper and turquoise, but in this case the turquoise was a composite of small pieces ground together and coated in resin, then worked together with the copper to give the effect of a turquoise river snaking through a copper desert.

"I know I didn't," Sadie said. "In fact, I was kind of surprised when I called you that you weren't already here yourself."

"I do tend to get in here a few times a week," Roz admitted. "So you're lucky I haven't been here already today."

"You're not really here a few times a week," Sadie said, looking at her friend.

Roz raised her hands. "Guilty!" she said. "But I don't come in here to *shop*. I think of it more like a museum. Just one where you sometimes get to buy the things you see."

"Fred and Debbie do carry beautiful things here," Sadie agreed, as they stepped in the door.

As they did, Debbie Sunshine looked up from behind the counter. Tall and lanky with hippie-styled gray hair, she gave a big grin at the sight of the two of them.

"My favorite customer!" she said. "And my favorite fellow shop owner!"

"I won't tell anyone else on the block you said that," Sadie said. "Especially not Fred."

"Well," Debbie said, laughing at Sadie's joke, "Fred does own the shop with me. But I think he knows he's in a category by himself."

"I've always thought you're both in a category of your own," Sadie said.

"That's what I keep trying to tell Fred," Debbie said.

She turned to Roz. "And it's been a little while since I've seen you, I think," she said.

"A whole two days!" Roz answered, with a laugh.

"Well, believe it or not, we do have a few things that are new that might be of interest to you," Debbie said, leading them over to a nearby case. In the upper corner a beautiful hand-lettered sign read "Steven Owens: Handmade Gems."

"Oh!" Roz said, walking past the other cases, which were also filled with beautiful necklaces, bangles, and rings, to see.

"You told me that he was going to bring out a new collection." She peered through the glass. "These are wonderful," she said.

"Aren't they?" Debbie agreed. "Fred and I go all over the Southwest, looking for the most talented jewelry designers we can. And, of course, I wanted to encourage a hometown designer if we were able to. Especially one like Steven, who has always been such a help around the store. So I didn't mind loaning him the space in the back to do some of his work. But it came as a very pleasant surprise when he started showing us what he was making, and we realized that we have a great jewelry designer right here in our own backyard."

"It is just as strong as anything I've ever seen in here," Roz said, still looking down at the new collection, which was arranged carefully on squares of black velvet, surrounded by brightly colored scarves.

Sadie wasn't an expert on jewelry, but she liked what she saw: interesting designs, mostly following what seemed to be Navajo patterns, but with some modern twists. "Now, Steven has been working for you in the shop, as well," Sadie said, "hasn't he? Is he here now?"

Debbie smiled and tilted her head toward the back room. "He is," she said. "But I'm afraid he's not on the clock. He did a shift earlier this morning, and now he's just getting a few hours in on his own work before he takes off."

"Well, do you think he'd be willing to talk with us about a few of the pieces in this collection?" Roz asked. "I'm very interested in several of them, and I'd love to hear directly from the artist what inspired them."

"Let me check," Debbie said, disappearing behind the seventies-style tie-dyed curtain that blocked the view of the back from the shop floor.

"That was good thinking," Sadie told Roz. "Thank you."

"Try not to sound so surprised that I have a good idea from time to time," Roz told her, with a friendly poke in the ribs.

A moment later, Deb came back out through the wildly colored curtains, with a middle-aged man in tow. He was wearing a denim shirt and jeans, and had powerful shoulders, although he also had a bit of a belly. His hair was salt-and pepper gray, and cut short, almost as if he'd been in the military.

"Roz," Deb said. "This is Steven."

Steven stuck his hand across the counter to shake Roz's. "I think I've helped you before," he said, recognizing her from her earlier visits to the shop.

"I'm sure you have," Roz said with a smile. "But not with your own designs. These are beautiful."

A shy grin lit up Steven's face. "Thank you," he said, ducking his head.

"And I'm Sadie," Sadie said, extending her own hand to shake his.

"Nice to meet you," Steven said politely.

Roz leaned onto the display case, and tapped on it, pointing down to the jewelry inside. "I was just telling Debbie that your work is some of the best I've ever seen," she said. "And as you know from all of my visits to the shop, I've seen quite a bit of it."

"Well, that's very kind of you," Steven said.

"Can you tell us a little bit about what inspires you?" Sadie asked. "It seems as if there's native influence in the design."

Steven nodded vigorously. "Yes, ma'am," he said. "I'm glad you saw that. Sometimes if people aren't familiar with the history and culture of native people, they think I'm just doing something that's a little wild and crazy on my own, because they haven't seen much like it before. But to me, it's all part of a long tradition. I don't pretend to have made this all up on my own. And I try to work with the traditions that inspire me with a great deal of respect. Because they're not just about decoration. They're about history, and spirit."

"That's beautiful," Roz said.

"Well, native people are beautiful," Steven said. "And so is their culture, and their history."

"It seems like all this is personal for you," Sadie said. "Do you have native ancestors in your background?"

Steven shook his head. "A lot of people will claim that," he said. "And a lot of times you have to wonder if that's even true. But I don't have any native ancestors in my background. At least not that I know of. It's just something I got interested in when I was younger. I guess I was always kind of interested in history myself. I remember other kids were always fascinated in finding an arrowhead out in the woods. And some of them did. They were real interested in collecting them. But I guess I was interested in a different way. I was curious about who made them. And that got me wondering what else they made. And that changed the whole way I look at the world."

"I can see that," Roz said, gazing down at the beautiful jewelry he'd created.

"Sometimes I'm not sure how to think about it," he said. "Because it's not my own history. I don't want to pretend to be something I'm not. Or to take something that's not mine. But I hope what I'm doing is a way to honor native culture, even though it's not part of my blood. That's the way I mean it, anyhow."

"Then you must always enjoy the exhibit of local artifacts that Kimama puts on at the library," Sadie said, watching Steven closely.

As she said this, his eyes lit up with what seemed like genuine enthusiasm. "I do love those," he said. "Ever since the very first one. I think I might actually be kind of a superfan. I even remember which pieces were there the year before, and which are new, and which haven't come back again. If they made playing cards of the pieces, I'd probably be collecting them."

"I can think of worse ways to spend your time," Roz said with a grin. "At least you'd be learning something."

"That's right," Steven said, nodding enthusiastically. "But not just learning. I don't only love those pieces because of what they tell me about history. I mean, that's important too, I guess. But I love them because they make me feel something."

"What do you mean?" Sadie asked.

Steven glanced down at his jewelry under the lit glass.

"It's hard to explain," he said. "It's almost like, if I could tell you what it was, then I wouldn't need to make the thing to show you. But it's something different than I ever feel any other place. The patterns and designs are so different from anything I ever see anywhere else. And they make me feel a completely new way."

"So what are some of the pieces you've liked most at the library?" Sadie asked.

"That's a good question," he said. "Of course, I think probably almost everybody has a soft spot for Najavo turquoise. There's just nothing else like it."

"I have quite a bit of it myself," Roz said. "And you're right. I find I can't resist it because each piece of stone is so unique. Even if you find the pattern again, you can never be sure you're going to get that specific color or that specific pattern. And some of them are just so striking. It's like you've got a miniature mountain range on your wrist, with little rivers and creeks of black minerals running through them."

"They do look like mountains, don't they?" Steven said. "When the piece is set natural, instead of all sanded down into place. I never thought of that before."

"I can't help seeing it," Roz said. "I don't know why. I'd just love to see one in real life. Can you imagine that? An actual mountain, made of actual turquoise?"

"Or a whole range of them...," Steven said, his eyes going faraway at the prospect.

"There are some beautiful pieces in the exhibit," Sadie said, trying to bring the conversation back to the topic she was interested in.

Steven nodded, as if to shake the idea of full-size mountains of turquoise out of his head. "There are," he said. "And not just the Navajo. There's some beautiful silverwork there too. And beading from the Plains peoples. Some of the beadwork is actual jewelry, you know, necklaces and bracelets, and some decorative elements to be worked into hair, bands and pins. But they've also got a ceremonial breastplate that's beaded, that I can never help thinking of as a kind of jewelry. Those glass beads are just so beautiful, especially when they're worked by someone who had an artist's eye for it. I think I've learned just as much of my craft from looking at beadwork as I have studying more traditional jewelry. I mean, there's one jacket in there that's got a whole sunset worked out on the back, in about a hundred different colors of beads. It might as well be Tiffany glass. It sure gives you a different idea about what can be accomplished with little tiny scraps of color. Which is what a lot of jewelry-making is about, in a way. I mean, at least once you get into working with gems and colored stones."

"That makes a lot of sense," Roz said. She pointed at one of his pieces in the case, a thick cuff in which he'd created the illusion of sun casting light over water with tiny flecks of white, yellow, orange, and blue stone. "I think maybe I see some of that in this one."

"You do, indeed," Steven said. "I was actually thinking of that jacket I mentioned when I got the inspiration for this one."

"Could I see it more closely?" Roz asked.

Helpfully, Debbie unlocked the case, pulled out the velvet display, and laid it in front of Roz.

An instant later, the sunset was gleaming from Roz's wrist.

"What do you think?" she asked Sadie, turning her wrist this way and that to show the cuff off to the greatest advantage.

Sadie had to admit Steven was a talented artist. Depending on which way Roz turned the cuff, the stones seemed to be depicting the first light of dawn, or the last light of the evening. And in any case, the image was always strikingly beautiful.

"You do wonderful work," Sadie told Steven.

"I mean, what do you think of how it looks on me?" Roz said, giving Sadie a poke in the ribs.

"Is there anything that doesn't look better when you're wearing it?" Sadie asked her friend with a grin.

"I knew I liked you," Roz said. She looked back at the bracelet. "My only question is how I've managed to live so long without it."

She glanced at Deb. "I'm afraid to look at the price tag," she said. "Should I be?"

Deb gave a noncommittal smile. "We try to keep everything in our shop in a range that's within reach of our customers," she said. "But it is an extraordinary piece. There's no doubt about that."

"But I could negotiate with you," Steven said. "If you decide it's something you feel seriously about."

Deb laughed. "I keep telling him he's got to stop negotiating with customers if he wants to start a real business."

"And I keep telling her that I don't make my jewelry to make money. I make it to make people happy," Steven said.

"It definitely makes me happy," Roz said. "But that's worth something too." She pulled the cuff off and looked at the tag.

Her eyebrows jumped.

"I'll need to think about that a bit before I get it," she said. "It's not the kind of thing I can do simply as an impulse purchase."

"Well, I could...," Steven began.

Roz raised her hand. "I don't want a discount," she said. "It's worth at least as much as you've priced it at. But I would like you to do me the favor of holding it for me for a day while I think it over. Would you be willing to do that?"

Steven nodded eagerly.

"Wonderful," Roz said. "I very much suspect that I'll be back here tomorrow, to make a purchase then."

She collected her bag from the counter, pleased, but Sadie wasn't done yet. She tapped on the glass over a design that featured a drum and a flute.

"And you're a musician too, aren't you?" she asked. "I know you're a friend of Spike Harris."

"Yes, ma'am," Steven said, drawing himself up with a proud grin. "In fact, I think that may be my answer to my favorite part of the exhibit over at the library this year. They're going to be showing a native instrument that's never been shown before. But I've seen it," he added, his eyes aglow. "They asked Spike to write a song on it, to help celebrate the collection. So he's been over there, trying to figure out how to play on it. And I got to go over there one day this week. I'd be scared to death to play on something that old, but Spike told me in a lot of orchestras people play instruments that were made at least that long ago.

"He even played on it a bit for me. It sounded real pretty too. It's got a real clear sound, but also different. Like nothing I ever heard before. It gave me the same feeling native designs sometimes do, that there's a way to see things from a different point of view. Even if you don't know exactly what that is, at first."

Could Steven have been the one who damaged the instrument? She studied his face carefully for any sign of the nervousness or signs of deceit she would expect to see if he was lying: not being able to meet her eyes, or strange little hand gestures. But he met her eyes steadily, and then nodded, only breaking her gaze to look up to the side, as if he was trying to remember something.

"So you heard about what happened to the instrument then," Sadie said. "From Spike?"

Steven's eyes grew wide, but not, as far as Sadie could see, wary. "'Happened'?" he repeated. "Did something happen to it?"

"It was damaged," Sadie said. "Badly."

Steven's face twisted in disappointment that quickly turned to indignation. "How badly?" he said. "What happened?"

"We're not sure of that yet," Sadie said. "The whole face of the instrument was separated from the belly."

"So it can't be played again?" Steven said. "That's awful. I was one of the last people to hear it."

"We're hoping to repair it," Sadie said. "And if that's possible, I'm very much hoping it will be able to be played again."

Steven drew in a deep breath, shaking his head. "Who would do a thing like that?" he asked. "This is one of the things that's so hard to think about, if you start learning about native history. There was so much beauty here. Such amazing civilizations. And it's all been lost. The Comanche were probably the best military riders in history. They could ride in formation in a perfect circle, and tighten and tighten it, at full gallop, until they could reach whatever they'd trapped inside.

"The mound builders built some of the largest structures the world has ever seen," he said. "Massive. Ambitious. Beautiful. Full of history and meaning. But most of them were dug up by curious Europeans. And most of the artifacts those people found in the mounds didn't even make it into museums. They wound up in private collections, or they got lost entirely. It's always made me feel sick to think about everything that's been lost.

"Not to mention what it would feel like to have that happen to us," he said. "I remember one native jewelry maker who was showing me how to do a few techniques I hadn't been able to get the hang of. I'm not sure how we got to talking about it, but I'll never forget what he said. I was saying how it made me sick that we couldn't even go see any of this history in museums. And he asked me how it would feel if someone took my grandfather's bones and clothes and put them on display for everyone to see.

"I'd never thought of it that way before. I always figured it was good for people to go see things at the museum, learn about other people's history. But it's a lot more personal than I had thought about. And that's a different thing."

Sadie looked at Steven with sympathy, and some relief. She would have almost been able to understand his motivation, if he had tried to damage the instrument, given how hard Spike said he seemed to be working to try to take care of his family.

But from their conversation, Steven seemed for all the world to have the same kind of veneration for things of the past that had led her to open her antique store. She knew a kindred spirit when she heard one. And his concern, not just for the damaged instrument from the exhibit, but for the preservation of all kinds of native history, from jewelry techniques to burial mountains, seemed nothing but sincere.

Still, Sadie thought, he had been one of the last people to see the instrument before it was damaged. And according to Spike, he'd made it outside before Spike did. So maybe he'd seen something that could help them figure out who had damaged the instrument—and make sure that nothing else in the exhibit, or the library, suffered the same fate, or worse.

"Well, you're right that you were one of the last people to hear the instrument played before it was damaged," Sadie said. "Do you happen to remember anything at all that might be significant from that night? Did you notice anything unusual at the library?"

Steven pondered for a moment, then shook his head. "Nope," he said apologetically. "I'm afraid I can't. It just seemed like a regular night in Silver Peak. And that's always seemed like a good thing to me. You won't hear me complaining about good old peace and quiet."

"Or," Sadie probed, "on the street? Outside?"

Again, Steven shook his head. A bit more quickly, this time, Sadie thought with interest. "No, ma'am," he said. "Not that I remember."

"And did you just go on home from there?" Sadie asked.

Now Steven's brow furrowed. "I'm sorry," he said. "I don't remember."

"It was just a few nights ago," Sadie said. "Two days ago."

"Yeah," Steven said with an apologetic shrug. "I've got kind of a lot on my plate right now. Half the time I can't remember what I did in the morning by the afternoon."

"Sometimes you'll mow a lawn or two before you go home," Debbie suggested. "Did you stop by and do one of those?"

Steven shook his head. "There hasn't been as much of that work since fall set in," he said.

"Could you check your calendar?" Sadie asked. "If that wouldn't be too much trouble?"

She hadn't been certain if Steven was genuinely scatterbrained, or if he was trying to hide something. But now he wouldn't meet her eyes. And she got the distinct feeling that he wasn't telling her everything he knew. "I don't really keep a calendar," he said. "Sorry about that."

Without being asked, he started to scoop up the jewelry from the counter and replace it in the case. When it had all been stored back again under the glass, he took another quick glance at Roz and Sadie.

"It's been nice talking with you," he said. "But I do have some more work in the back. I hope you won't mind if I get back to it."

"Not at all," Roz said. "I can't wait to see what you're making back there."

"Thanks," Steven said, shuffling toward the curtain that hid the workshop from the retail space. "I'm sorry there wasn't more I could do to help."

"Oh, you've told us plenty," Sadie called after him. "For now."

14

"I LIKE DOING THIS," SADIE SAID. "LET'S FIND A WAY TO DO THIS for a living."

Riding behind her up the trail between the pines, Edwin laughed.

Ahead, her dog, Hank, romped happily through the trees, picking up all the messages left amidst the loamy soil of the forest and all the scents on the breeze that Sadie and Edwin could only guess at.

"I think it's called 'being a cowboy,'" Edwin said. "And I'm not sure you'd like some of the other parts of the job description."

"I bet I could rope a calf," Sadie teased back. "I've wrangled a toddler or two in my day."

"And more than a few high school students," Edwin teased. "But I'm not sure how you'd like the part about sleeping outside most nights. Or spending most of your life with a pack of unwashed, illiterate varmints."

"Varmints, you say?" Sadie asked. "Well, I guess I would have to think about that. It is a beautiful day today, though, isn't it?"

"Even this old litigator can't argue with that," Edwin said.

He looked up to take in the sweep of the high, blue Colorado sky. The mountains hung in the distance as they always did, like some kind of permanent movie backdrop. No matter how long Sadie lived in Colorado, she could never quite believe that they were real, or that they'd still be there the next day when she awoke. And they never stopped making her feel a little flutter in her stomach, and make her breath catch in her throat.

Kind of like the way seeing Edwin still gave her a pleasant thrill each time he came in the room, just the way it had when they had first dated so many years ago, as teenagers. Later, the two of them had gone off to live separate lives in other towns, but now life had brought them back together, here in Silver Peak.

Sadie took a long, deep breath of the crisp mountain air. It was always a bit cooler here, outside of town, than it was among the paved streets and sidewalks of Silver Peak, even on the hottest dog days of summer. In fact, the hotter things got, the more likely Sadie was to run into one of her neighbors sheltering from the blaze among the shade of the pine woods when she and Hank, or she and Edwin, or all three of them took one of their customary rambles through the semi-wilderness.

But today, she thought she felt an even deeper twinge of cold in the air—a hint of the real bite of a chill that promised the coming winter, which would be on them sooner than they knew it, now that Thanksgiving was almost here. In a few weeks, or even sooner, it would be so cold that she wouldn't be able to enjoy the wind on her cheeks, or the feel of the sunshine falling on her shoulders. She'd have to be too bundled up, just to survive outside.

There was a certain charm to that too, though—she always liked the feeling that she'd survived something, just by going outside. For the first European settlers in the area, she knew, that had genuinely been the case. They hadn't had warm houses to return to when they first arrived, with furnaces and electric lights. Surviving the Colorado winter had been much more serious than a game to them. And the sad truth was that some of them hadn't made it. So Sadie always felt lucky to have the thrill of breathing in the truly cold air of a Colorado winter—and even luckier in the moment when she got to step out of it, into her own warm and cozy home.

"It sounds like you just let a load off of your shoulders," Edwin said.

"I don't know," Sadie said. "I think I might just be taking a deep breath before I go at it from another angle."

Up ahead, but just out of sight, Hank burst into enthusiastic barking.

"What in the world?" Sadie said, spurring Scout on. Gladly, the chestnut gelding broke into a brief canter, seeming more than a little disappointed when Sadie reined him in again at her first sight of Hank, who was still yelping energetically at the foot of one of the giant pines that stood particularly close to the rocky trail they had chosen to follow that day.

"Hank!" Sadie said. "What are you going on about?"

Hank continued to energetically communicate to his mistress whatever it was that had caught his eye in the upper branches of the trees, but whatever it was had gotten too high up for Sadie's eyes to make out. Either that, or whatever had set Hank off was already long gone.

"Hank," Sadie said a bit more forcefully. When that failed to get his attention, she whistled. "Come on."

But before she could extract Hank from whatever protective mission he had appointed himself to, she heard Edwin's footsteps behind her. She twisted around in her saddle to see Edwin's horse riderless, gazing absently into the woods beyond the path, and Edwin on foot, diving into the brush near where Hank was still yapping.

"Edwin?" Sadie asked.

Edwin disappeared behind a tree. She expected him to emerge any moment on the other side, but instead he completely vanished. When he finally did emerge, he was carrying a quickly improvised bundle of black-eyed Susans, one of Sadie's favorite flowers.

At the sight of Edwin with the blooms, Hank immediately stopped barking, and loped happily back to the path, as proudly as if he were carrying a prize pheasant in his jaws like one of the king's retrievers.

Edwin patted him on the head as he passed him, then walked up to Scout and raised the bouquet, offering it to Sadie.

Sadie looked from Edwin to Hank, puzzled. "That can't have been what Hank was making all that racket about," she said.

"Well, you see," Edwin said, "Hank and I have been doing some extracurricular work together. Retrievers are wired to bring back treasures to their masters, you know. I just had to train him to recognize some of his mistresses' favorite flowers."

He raised the bouquet toward Sadie again with a grin, but she still didn't take them.

"That's impossible," she said. "You did not."

Edwin shrugged with a mischievous look. "As a judge," he said, "I always try to let the evidence speak for itself."

"And as a researcher of antiques, I can tell you that not everything is what it first seems," Sadie teased back.

Edwin nodded to give her the point. "Still," he said. "It's customary, when a gentleman offers a lady flowers, for her to take them. Unless he's done something to displease her. In which case I can give them to Hank."

He lifted the bouquet over Scout's swayed back again. This time, Sadie leaned down to collect them, and gave him a quick peck on the cheek as a reward.

Edwin beamed with pleasure, and practically bounded back to his own horse, which he swung up onto with all the energy and grace she remembered from their teen years.

At a signal from him, his horse trotted up the few yards to catch up with Sadie, and they continued along the trail side by side, following after the retreating form of Hank's golden tail as it wagged behind him through the evergreens.

"So what's on your mind?" Edwin asked. "I know you were looking forward to working with Kimama on that exhibit over at the library."

"I was," Sadie said.

At the tone of her voice, Edwin turned to get a look at her face. "That doesn't sound exactly like enjoyment to me," he said.

"It's not," she said.

"Is something wrong?" he asked.

Sadie nodded. "More than one thing, I'm afraid," she said, and briefly explained to him about the breakage of the instrument, Kimama's history with it, the second break-in at the library, and her visits to the Granby family, and even Steven, over at Bless Our Souls.

When she was finished, to her surprise, Edwin grinned. "This is what I've always liked about you, Sadie Speers," he said. "I can't leave you alone for two days without you getting mixed up in some whole big story."

"Well, I guess I'm glad you're amused," Sadie told him. "But to me, it's not just a story. It's causing a lot of trouble for a lot of people I care about. And I'd sure like to see the end of that."

"I can understand that," Edwin said, his expression turning sober. "I like how thoroughly you give yourself to your loved ones. I always have."

Sadie smiled at him.

"Although I do have to say, a lot of them make great stories," he added.

Sadie pretended to take a gentle swat at him, but their two horses trotted just too far away from one another for her to reach.

"So," Edwin said, as he ducked away, "it sounds like you're getting an education in the history of native people in this part of the territory."

"I'm trying to," Sadie said, thinking back on how many of the conversations she'd had recently had come to an abrupt end when she tried to learn anything about the history of the broken instrument—either where it had originally come from, or what had even happened to it right there in the Silver Peak Library that week. "It's turning out to be a lot harder than I thought."

"What do you mean?" Edwin asked.

"Well, the original plan was just for me to help Kimama discover a bit more about the artifact, so that we would have something to share with library patrons when they visited the exhibit," Sadie said. "But the instrument is so unusual that even the expert I brought in from Denver hasn't been able to give us a conclusive answer to the simplest questions, like which group of people it was most likely associated with."

"It sounds like you've got something special on your hands," Edwin said.

"That's one word for it," Sadie said. "It's also the word my mother used to use when she was talking about a particularly difficult child."

Edwin laughed. "Well, the most special things aren't always the easiest to understand at first glance," he said, with a knowing look at her.

"What are you trying to say?" she teased back. "You'd better not be calling me 'special.' At least not the way my mother meant it."

Edwin smiled and held his hands up in surrender. Then he returned his hands to the horse and looked again at Sadie.

"The problem isn't just identifying the instrument, now. We're also trying to find out what happened to it. And that's also far more difficult than I thought it would be. I can't even get the Granby family to tell me the story of how it came into their hands."

"A lot of times those kinds of stories get lost over the years," Edwin suggested, as the hooves of their horses clopped on peacefully along the stone and packed dirt of the forest path.

Sadie shook her head firmly. "Not this one," she said. "Or at least not all of it. Beverly Granby knows something about that instrument that she's not telling. It might not be the whole story, but it's definitely more than I know."

"That doesn't surprise me," Edwin said, the tone of his voice slightly sad.

Sadie looked at him with surprise. He was always supportive and curious about anything she was interested in or working on.

But he didn't always show a lot of emotion. And she was surprised that this story would move him any more than the many others she'd told him over their times together.

"What do you mean?" she asked.

"Well, I don't know if I've ever talked with you about this before," Edwin said. "But I did have several cases regarding native people cross my bench while I was a judge. And ever since then, native history and law regarding native people has been an interest of mine."

"I didn't know that," Sadie said.

Edwin nodded. "The legal issues involved are very intriguing to me," he said. "It's a very knotty question, what it means to have nations that exist within the boundaries of another nation. Especially when one of the nations is so much more powerful than the other. Legal scholars have been wrestling with it for years."

"Since the United States was first formed," Sadie said.

"Believe it or not, even before that," Edwin told her. "Europeans spent an enormous amount of time trying to figure out what was the most ethical way to deal with the people they were meeting in the new world. Especially in the Church."

"That's fascinating," Sadie said. "I thought the conquistadors pretty much just conquered everyone they could find."

"They did," Edwin said. "In practice, that's often what happened. Since they had horses and guns, Europeans were tough to defeat. And many natives died from European diseases after we first arrived. But there were a lot of Church thinkers back in Europe writing law that was supposed to help us better understand what it meant to be human, and what we owed to our fellow people."

"I guess we must have recognized them as nations," Sadie said. "Because we made treaties with them."

"That's right," Edwin said. "Although we didn't keep many of them. Not until we'd taken pretty much everything we wanted."

"But all that's been over for years," Sadie said. "It's a sad story, but it happened so long ago."

"I'm always surprised when I think about how close it actually is," Edwin said. "We gave away the last large block of native land to white settlers in 1889, with the Sooner Land Rush. That's just over a hundred years ago. Would you believe that Geronimo was still alive in 1909?"

Sadie shook her head. "Wow," she said.

Edwin nodded. "And it's still very much with us today," he said. "What really troubles me is the problem of justice on reservations."

"I don't know anything about that," Sadie said. "Don't they have their own courts?"

"Yes," Edwin said. "But they only have jurisdiction over their own people, on their own soil."

"Is that any different from how other courts work?" Sadie asked. "American courts don't get to try French people, unless they've committed a crime here."

"As usual, you've put your finger right on the problem," Edwin said.

"What's that?" Sadie asked, surprised.

"Well," Edwin said, "France controls its own borders. You have to have a passport and clear customs to go in and out of the country."

"You don't have to do that to visit the Navajo Nation," Sadie said, remembering back to a visit she'd made there, years ago, when her children were younger.

"That's right," Edwin said. "Because they're contained within the borders of the United States. In many places, you can simply drive right into and out of them. No passport, nothing. But native people don't have the same jurisdiction over those visitors that the United States has over visitors from France who commit a crime."

"They don't?" Sadie asked.

Edwin shook his head. "No," he told her. "Their police, and their courts, only have jurisdiction over their own people. They can't try visitors for crimes in their territories."

"So what happens if someone who isn't a native commits a crime on a reservation?" Sadie asked.

Edwin took a deep, weary breath. "In theory," he said, "it becomes the responsibility of the US authorities in the surrounding area. But in practice, you can imagine how it goes. Police forces and prosecutors are already stretched thin. They're not able to handle everything that's already thrown at them. So they're not eager to take on cases in an area they're not familiar with. And they're especially not eager to take on cases that are hard to win—and it's hard to win cases when you're not familiar with the area."

"That's terrible," Sadie said.

"And it has some very sad consequences," Edwin said. "Especially in attacks against women. The rate of visitors attacking native women on reservations is very high, in both the United States and Canada."

"And there's nothing we can do about it?" Sadie asked.

"I'm sure there are things we can do," Edwin said. "But finding healing, and real justice, will require a lot of time, and a lot of commitment. I think maybe that's why these questions mean so much to me."

"Why is that?" Sadie asked.

"I always think about the part in the Bible where Jesus says that even the worst sinners still take care of their own," Edwin said. "He says that we can't take credit for caring for our own people and our own families, because even the worst people in the world still try to do that."

"I remember that," Sadie said. The passage was in Matthew, if she remembered correctly.

"And He tells us in other places that the real measure of a person is how they treat the people who aren't like them. My mind always goes back to that," Edwin says. "That the measure of our character isn't how we treat the people who are like us, but the ones who aren't. I think we can learn a lot about who we are by how we treat people who don't have as much power as we do."

"I think that's true," Sadie said.

"And I wonder," Edwin said thoughtfully, "if that might be some small piece of what you're running into here. People don't always want to talk about native history, because it's not always pretty. People have spent a lot of time trying to forget it."

"There's so much of history that's hidden," Sadie mused. "That's one of my favorite things to do with antiques, to uncover history that's gotten lost. But I guess not everyone wants every part of history to be uncovered. In fact, some people may have a lot of reasons for not wanting certain things to come to light."

"I always thought there are as many ways to look at history as there are people in the world," Edwin said. "One of the things I saw over and over again as a judge is that even people who were in the same place at the same time saw very different things."

"You mean the way I'll be staring at the antiques in the windows while you're looking at which model of car is coming down the street?" Sadie joked.

"Well, that's a bit more pleasant example than the ones you normally see coming into court," Edwin said. "But, yes. You've got the gist of it."

"And I imagine that's probably true for a lot of native history," Sadie mused.

"Absolutely," Edwin said. His tone brightened with interest. "That's another thing that's amazing about studying native history. Whole civilizations rose and fell here in the Americas, all with incredible stories.

"Like the introduction of the horse," he said, patting his horse's flank. "Before the Europeans arrived, there were no horses in America. So the Great Plains tribes that became such gifted riders—all of that culture developed *after* the first contact with Europeans. And it completely changed traditional ways of life that had been going on for centuries."

"That is amazing," Sadie agreed. "And it wasn't just what we had to teach them," she added, remembering what Dr. Gramas had told her earlier. "They gave us potatoes, and tomatoes. And maybe even a foundational idea for the Constitution."

"And gold," Edwin added. "You know all the beautiful gilding on European palaces and churches? Most of that is American gold. We took so much of it out of the Americas that it actually changed the entire monetary system of Europe. And parts of Asia and Africa too."

"It's incredible how different history looks," Sadie mused, "depending on what vantage point you take."

"It is," Edwin said. "It's part of why I always try to think of things from the other person's point of view. Because I know I can't see everything. So I need to hear what other people think, as well, if I want to understand the world."

"That's true even when it's just two people talking on the street," Sadie said.

Edwin nodded. "That's what I've found," he said.

"And it's probably just as true with family history," Sadie went on, thinking back to the Granbys again. "The story changes, depending on who's telling it."

"It may be even more true with family history than with the history of whole countries," Edwin said. "At least when historians write history, there are some checks and balances. People working to get the facts right, and other people making sure they have. That kind of work doesn't usually get done on a family's history. So all that comes down through the generations is whatever story they want to tell."

"And nothing about anything they don't want to tell," Sadie finished for him.

15

———

"THIS IS VERY INTERESTING," SADIE SAID, LOOKING OVER THE
face of the giant, dusty old clock Ardis Fleagle had just brought in
and deposited on the counter of the Antique Mine the following
morning.

She *was* interested, and under normal circumstances, she
might actually have been *very* interested. But the fact of the matter
was that he had interrupted her just as she had begun an Internet
search for the history of the Granby family. The bell had rung
announcing his entrance to the shop as the first tantalizing
returns of the search had flashed up on her screen, and now it was
everything she could do not to tell Ardis he was going to have to
hold his horses for a minute while she took a look at them.

If she did that, though, she would leave him literally holding
the horses—there were several of them painted on the face of the
clock, representing the various seasons, all with the peaks of what
were recognizable as Colorado mountains visible in the distance:
a white pony cantering through a field of snow, a chestnut mare
snacking on some spring clover, a palomino carrying a rider
through the lush green of a summer field, and a proud black
Arabian kicking up colored leaves with his hooves.

"It's amazing what you find in the walls of houses," Ardis said. "I would have said I'd seen it all. Fishing lures. Jewelry. Old newspapers. But this, I have to say, is something new."

Ardis was a contractor in town, so he knew a lot more about what was to be found in the walls of Silver Peak's old buildings than just about anyone in town. And a lot of what he knew, he shared with Sadie. He loved history just as much as she did, but his specialty was the "bones" of old houses, and vintage restoration practices. When it came to dealing with smaller, individual pieces, like the one he had just deposited on her counter, along with what looked to be a pile of construction dust, he brought those to Sadie, both for her expert opinion, and for her knack at shining them back into good-as-new quality.

"Well, this is hand-painted, I can tell you that much," Sadie said, wiping away the construction dust from the face of the clock so she could get a better look at the images of the horses below. "Probably during the craze for ceramic painting at the beginning of the last century."

"They look like pretty good paintings to me," Ardis said. Then he grinned. "But I've got to say, I've always preferred looking at a good horse than at a lot of those portraits of crown princes they seem to have hanging up at some museums."

"You say you found this in a wall?" Sadie said.

Ardis nodded. "Yep," he said. "It was the funniest thing. I couldn't figure out why there was this corner jutting out from the wall. The owners thought it must be a structural element, but when I began taking it down to the studs on the floor below, I could see that wasn't the case. There was just no reason for it. So we decided it had to go. And when one of my guys went through the plaster with a crowbar, this was the first thing he saw."

"It's impressive," Sadie said.

"I'm just glad he stopped," Ardis said. "You give the right kind of a man a crowbar and a wall to take down, and it can be hard to put the brakes on."

"Well, I'm sure your client will be very happy you found this," Sadie said.

"That's what I'm thinking," Ardis said. "But I'd like it to be in a little better shape before they see it. And it'd be nice to know some history, if you're able to dig any up for me."

"I'd be glad to," Sadie said.

Ardis tipped his painter's cap back on his head in a courtly gesture. "Much appreciated," he said. "You know, I'd love to stay and talk…"

"Oh, please," Sadie said, her heart secretly glad for the chance to get back to her own work. "Don't have any worries on my account."

Ardis patted the clock. "Thanks," he said.

"I'll call you as soon as it's done," Sadie said, picking up the clock to carry it back to the workroom, where she would accomplish its transformation.

When she returned to her computer at the front of the store, her eyes quickly scanned down the results that had come up after she had typed in the Granby family name, along with *Silver Peak, Colorado*. Using that name, she did find a few references to what looked like the small camp outside town that Beverly had mentioned, including a few grainy pictures of small children blinking at the camera while bearded men, their eyes shaded by large hats, squinted back at it alongside them.

But there was no mention of the old mill that Beverly had mentioned. Sadie knew the site well, though, and had even been out there a few times herself, because the picturesque spot was popular as a destination for picnics and hikes in town. It wasn't a figment of Beverly's imagination. But did the Granby family have anything to do with it?

Curious, Sadie typed in *Silver Peak* and *old mill.*

Her screen filled with blog entries, and a wide band of amateur and professional photographs that had been snapped at the spot, which looked just as she had remembered it—and probably as it had over a hundred years ago, when it had first been built and provided important power for the town's first residents to grind the fruit of their labors in the fields.

Further down the page, though, she did find a blog containing a longish-looking article on the mill's local history.

But just as she clicked through on it, the bell over her door rang again.

It was all Sadie could do not to let out an audible groan as her next customer walked into the shop.

But as soon as she saw who it was, her face brightened.

"Genevieve!" she said. "It's lovely to see you!"

Genevieve Lakier smiled back at her as she came up to the counter, a pair of beautiful earrings swinging from each ear under her curly red hair. The earrings were a beautiful verdigris turquoise, over wrought metal punched with a pattern of vines that let through both sunshine and shadow. She was one of Sadie's regular customers: a mom with a young daughter, who loved to look at antiques whenever she could get some time to herself.

"You're not so bad to look at yourself," she said. "How have things been going?"

"Good," Sadie said, pushing her computer to the side to give Genevieve her full attention. "And what brings you here today?"

"Well," Genevieve said, looking around at the tempting displays that surrounded her, "usually I'm here to browse, as you know. But today, I'm on a mission."

"That sounds exciting," Sadie said.

"I may be making it out to be a bit more exciting than it actually is," Genevieve said. "But I don't think that's always a bad thing. Always good to keep a sense of adventure in life, right?"

"That's how I feel, anyway," Sadie said.

"Well," Genevieve said, depositing her purse on the counter, "everybody knows that Jeanne Sweeting is the expert on event planning in this town. But I think I told you I used to do a bit of it myself, before my husband and I moved here to Silver Peak."

Sadie nodded. "I'll always remember your telling me about that group of insurance salesmen who insisted that you provide them with full-size potted palm trees for one of their banquets."

"That's right," Genevieve said, laughing. "Along with real fire in the torches. But to their credit, they didn't blink when I presented them with the bill for the damage one of those palms sustained when one of their members decided to put a torch to it."

"Now, see," Sadie said. "There's an adventure. Right in the middle of an insurance salesmen's banquet."

Genevieve's brows drew together. "Actually," she said. "I think maybe their problem was they didn't feel they were getting enough adventure. So they decided to make their own, by causing trouble. Which to my mind is a very different thing."

Sadie smiled. "I see what you mean," she said.

"Right?" Genevieve said. "And you can probably see why after I left that job, I figured I was pretty much done with event planning for the rest of my life."

"I can see how you might feel that way," Sadie agreed.

"Especially if I tell you that story was only one among many," Genevieve went on.

"I believe it," said Sadie.

"However...," Genevieve said, with a comically ominous pause.

Sadie raised her eyebrows at the suspense.

"Somehow," Genevieve said, "word got out to Kimama."

"About the businessman who singed the palm trees?" Sadie asked, confused.

"About the fact that I have a background in event planning," Genevieve said. "And you know how Kimama is."

Sadie grinned as the pieces clicked into place. "Yes, I do," she said.

"Well," Genevieve said with a dramatic sigh, "now she's got me helping out with this event at the library this week."

"You have my condolences," Sadie said. "Although I suspect that, as a citizen of Silver Peak, I'm actually going to feel lucky that she managed to get you involved. So should I go to the event expecting to see torches and palm trees?"

"No," Genevieve said decisively. "But I would like to have a few other items on hand. And as the event planner for the library, I'm afraid to tell you that our budget is small. So instead of being an actual customer this morning, what I'm hoping you might be willing to do is to temporarily lend us some of your merchandise.

Of course, that will serve as a form of advertising for your shop—
and for the items."

"That only seems fair," Sadie said. "The library has lent so
much to me. Why wouldn't I be glad to lend something to them?"

Genevieve beamed.

"What are you looking for in particular?" Sadie asked her.

"I don't want to take the focus off of native history," Genevieve
said. "But I'd like to give everybody else a sense of how their history
fits into it. So I was hoping that you might have some items from
around that time that could give people a better feel for the lives
of the early settlers. And since there are so many art objects in the
exhibit, I thought it might be good to focus on antique crafts. I
know you've got that big stack of quilts in the back..."

Sadie smiled and nodded, pointing down the aisle Genevieve
had mentioned with an open hand. "They're all yours," she said.
"Take whatever you want. I'd just ask you to let me make a list
before you take them."

"A library card, if you will," Genevieve said.

"I guess so," Sadie said with a smile as Genevieve headed back
to investigate the quilts.

Then Sadie turned back to her computer screen. The article
on the mill history was just as informative as she'd hoped, full of
interesting details about the place of the mill in the town's history,
and the personal lives of the mill's owners. And, just as Beverly
said, it mentioned that the original owner had a son who had later
started a successful construction business. But their name wasn't
Granby. It was Barnhill.

That only made sense, Sadie reasoned. That far back, there
would have been all kinds of other names that were associated

with the family, many of which got lost or changed as family members were married and went on to start their own families. And it gave her another idea.

She typed *Granby* and *Barnhill* and *Silver Peak* into the search engine. This time, she hit the site of a local genealogist who had apparently done some work on the family, not as a member of it, but because of their importance in the local history. From it, Sadie could see the marriage that brought the Barnhill and Granby families together, and how it led from there right down to Candace Granby, through her mother, Beverly—and her mother, who, Sadie discovered, was named Etta.

But where was the connection to the native artifact? Sadie wondered.

So far, nothing she had learned about the family even breathed a word of any connection, although there must have been some, Sadie mused, especially, perhaps, with the original Granby settlers to the area, who lived in the encampment outside town where they might have been more likely to have contact with native people. But none of the articles, or the family tree, gave her any clue about what that connection might have been.

So Sadie tried another tack: searching various family names, along with the tag *native* or, bowing to the language that would probably have been used in the papers of the day, a hundred years ago, *Indian*. This yielded a handful of random hits, like for a native community center in a town called Barnhill, but nothing that showed any kind of link, however slim, to the Granby or Barnhill families—or any of the relatives Sadie sifted through from the family tree she'd also found.

But when Sadie got to Etta's grandmother, Anne Elizabeth, something strange happened. The search Sadie had run turned up practically nothing, just a handful of unrelated scraps. But an interesting query did appear at the top of the page. "Did you mean *Agatha Elizabeth*?" it asked, and promised thousands more returns.

"I think this should do it," Genevieve said, dropping a large heap of soft quilts on the counter beside Sadie's computer screen.

Sadie looked up. "Great, great," she said absently, eager to get back to the search.

Genevieve laughed and raised her eyebrows. "Well, where's my library card?" she said. "I don't want there to be any question about my turning anything back in overdue."

With effort, Sadie turned her attention away from the screen. "Of course," she said. "Let me just write something up..." Quickly, she pulled a purchase slip from under the counter and started a careful list of the quilts Genevieve had chosen. As she labeled them: sky blue star, red white burst, Irish chain, she couldn't help but get interested in Genevieve's selections.

"You've chosen some of my favorites," she observed.

"Well, you have beautiful taste," Genevieve said. "I probably could have just gone back there with my eyes closed and come up here with a whole other armful of gorgeous examples of early American handwork. But I did go to some effort to pick ones that seemed to have something in common with native design. Or even to have taken a page or two from it. The star quilts, for instance. I believe I heard once that those are a direct result of cultural exchange between native people and women settlers, who picked up their designs to use in their own quilts."

"I've heard the same thing," Sadie said. "And settlers weren't the only quilters. Native women also designed blankets out of scrap, using the same techniques. So the exchange went both ways."

"Do any of these fit that description?" Genevieve asked.

Sadie shook her head. "They're far more rare, as you can imagine," she said. "And when they do appear, they're a bit out of the range of my shop."

"I wonder if Kimama will ever rustle one up for us. In the library exhibit," Genevieve said.

"You could certainly talk to her about it," Sadie told her, making her final notation about the last quilt in the pile. "And these might serve as some good inspiration for her this year." She patted the pile of quilts, then pulled out several bags and settled each quilt carefully in, to protect them. Then she pushed the bags across the counter to Genevieve.

"There you go," she said. "They're due back the day after the exhibit comes down."

"Scout's honor," Genevieve said. "And if I'm late, I assume it's a quarter per day?"

"If you're late, cash won't work," Sadie said. "You'll have to pay off your debt by bringing me another antique quilt."

Genevieve laughed. "Well, that's a real threat," she said. "I'll have to make sure I'm right on time, then."

"I'm sure you will be," Sadie said. "I don't have any doubt about that."

"Well, thank you," Genevieve said. "I thank you, and the Silver Peak Library thanks you."

"I can't wait to see what you do with them," Sadie said, smiling as Genevieve headed out the door.

Finally alone again, Sadie turned back to the computer screen, and reread the query that had appeared at the top. She hadn't heard the name "Agatha Elizabeth" in any of the materials she'd seen so far about the Granby and Barnhill families. For all she knew, the information might just be a cluster of promotional materials and fan pages for some young starlet she'd never heard of, or some celebrity chef hawking a new diet.

But still, it was worth a try. After all, nothing else had worked yet.

Sadie clicked on the link.

The page filled up with a whole different set of search returns. But where Sadie had expected to see glossy advertising of some kind for an Internet-famous personality, instead, many of the entries still seemed to reference Silver Peak.

And, oddly, the images that flashed up along with them weren't modern. Instead, they were grainy, blurry, black-and-white—clearly antiques, and from a time when photography itself was still in its infancy.

Sadie clicked on the first link, an amateur historian's page with a picture of a gray-eyed young girl, aged about twelve or thirteen, who looked steadily back at the camera, her brown curls tied back in a large, pale bow, her clothes obviously ones that would have been considered fine at the time. "Agatha Elizabeth Barnhill" was emblazoned across the page, and written in India ink across the face of the photograph.

From the somewhat poorly written text, Sadie deduced that Agatha Elizabeth had grown up in Silver Peak. But there the story departed from anything Sadie had ever heard about Silver Peak history. Several newspaper clippings, which showed that the story must have been a big deal at the time, stated that Agatha Elizabeth had been kidnapped while out riding her pony through the woods outside town.

The contemporary newspapers, and the amateur's article, were all full of wild speculation. Some suggested that trappers might have made off with her. Others mentioned the presence of native riders who had been seen in the area in the days before Agatha's disappearance, but not afterward. One, in Denver, changed Agatha's age from thirteen to sixteen, and speculated that, petulant over her father's disapproval of a youthful romance, Agatha had decamped with her sweetheart to parts unknown.

As Sadie clicked through the various links, some of which repeated the original articles, and some of which added to them, she began to see the whole picture. The story had obviously been a huge one at the time—so big Sadie was surprised no memory of it seemed to have carried down to the present day. But as she followed it to its conclusion, she thought she began to see why. After weeks, and then months, of speculation, Agatha Elizabeth had never been found.

What had started out as the beginning of some kind of adventure ended in a tragedy with no answers. If that had happened to a young woman in town, Sadie could see why both the family, and the town might want to forget it.

But still, there was nothing to link this story to the instrument that had wound up in the Granby family's hands. In fact, if there was any suggestion that the family had lost a member to a kidnapping by natives, it was even more surprising that they would have kept a native artifact for so many years as a treasured family possession. Unless it was part of a different story, Sadie thought.

She checked her watch. The only way to dig any deeper than the articles on the Internet was to take Agatha Elizabeth's name over to the library, and dig through the actual Silver Peak archives to see what else she might find on Agatha Elizabeth's home turf, long after the sensationalistic news stories had died down.

But it was too late in the evening already. Even if she went over there, the library doors would be solidly closed, not to open until the following morning.

She'd have to wait until tomorrow.

16

Sadie trotted up the steps of the library, feeling a little thrill as a sweep of bright golden aspen leaves blew across the steps, and back out onto the surrounding lawns.

There was something so right about heading into the library when there was a chill in the air, to browse through the quiet stacks for adventures or new knowledge that could be discovered, page by page, during cozy nights as the days became shorter and more chilly outdoors.

But, of course, she wasn't here just to pick out an armload of books. She was on the trail of something she couldn't check out—whatever might lie in the Silver Peak archives concerning the mysterious girl who had disappeared from Silver Peak so many years ago.

As Sadie came through the front doors, she caught sight of Kimama. But instead of standing at the counter, greeting incoming guests as she usually did, Kimama's back was turned toward the door.

She turned back with a distracted look at the sound of the door thunking shut behind Sadie.

"Oh, hello," she said. She tried to give Sadie her usual warm greeting, but Sadie could see from Kimama's expression that the librarian was visibly perplexed.

Sadie's heart sank. Had there been yet another event at the library? And what had been damaged *this* time?

"Is everything okay?" Sadie asked.

Kimama squinted down at something on the floor behind the counter that Sadie couldn't see from her vantage point. She raised her hand and dropped it in a gesture of exasperation, or surrender. "I mean—I guess."

"What's wrong?" Sadie asked, scooting up to the counter so she could see. "Has something else been broken?"

Kimama shook her head. "Nothing's broken," she said. "I guess we can be grateful for that."

As Sadie peeked over the counter, she could see what Kimama had been looking down at: piles and piles of canned food, and James kneeling on the floor nearby, sorting it into even more piles. It looked like he'd gotten to work before even taking his coat off: He still wore the jeans jacket with the shearling collar that Sadie had gotten used to seeing slung over the back of whatever chair he happened to be working at.

"I guess you had a good take from the food drive," Sadie said approvingly.

"Well, that's the problem," Kimama said.

"Problem?" Sadie repeated, wondering how a bountiful food drive could possibly be considered a problem.

Kimama looked at her wearily. "I know," she said. "I never thought I'd hear myself complain that people had given too much food to the food drive. But that's not what I'm worried about."

"What are you worried about?" Sadie asked.

"Well," Kimama said, "none of this was here last night when we left."

James twisted to look back over his shoulder. "I always clean out the bins last thing before I go. And then I take the cans over to the grocery store to deliver them to the big drive collection point on the way home."

"And I usually check it on my way out to make sure it's done. Not that I can't trust James—he's always done a great job. But it's just a habit I got into," Kimama said, "noticing that one last thing that we finished up for the day, as I'm on my way out."

"And it was empty last night?" Sadie asked.

In unison, Kimama and James nodded.

Sadie looked at the cans around them. There must have been hundreds of them, along with all the bags they had originally come in, piled in an unwieldy stack of paper and plastic.

"It sounds like you had some very generous donors overnight, then," Sadie said.

"Well, that's the thing," Kimama said. "They shouldn't have been able to get in here."

"What do you mean?" Sadie asked.

"Some of the drops for the food drive are twenty-four hours," Kimama said. "And that only makes sense, because not everybody can get out and about to run errands like that during work hours. But I only signed up to take in donations during our normal working hours. The donation boxes are in our main foyer. You can push books into the return slot after hours. But the doors to the foyer itself are locked."

"If they're locked," Sadie asked, "then how in the world did all this food get into the boxes?"

"Because it wasn't locked," Kimama said.

"It was when we left," James insisted.

"That's right," Kimama said. "I locked it up myself when I went out. Just like I always do."

"And it was unlocked this morning?" Sadie asked.

"I guess it must have been," Kimama said. "Although I didn't notice when I came in. I just put the key in the lock like normal. But that would have worked even if it had been open."

"It's so strange," Sadie said, surveying the piles of canned peas and kidney beans. "But nothing was broken? Nothing was taken?"

"Not that I've discovered yet," Kimama said, with a somewhat grim set to her jaw. "But I hate the fact that the library doesn't seem to be secure."

"Of course," Sadie said.

"Especially with everything that's been happening," Kimama added.

"But maybe," Sadie said, "it explains some of what's been happening. Is this the first time that you've had a big overnight delivery like this?"

Kimama shook her head, thinking. But then her eyes widened. "No!"

"When?" Sadie asked.

"The day...," Kimama said, pausing as if to double-check her own reasoning in her head. "The day the instrument was broken. Do you remember that, James?"

James nodded cautiously.

"I thought James had forgotten to clear out the donation bin," Kimama said. "Because when I came in, it was already full to the brim, with a big donation of creamed corn and canned chili. Dozens and dozens of cans of it."

"I told you I'd taken it all in the night before," James said.

"I know," Kimama said, her voice slightly remorseful. "But I'm afraid I didn't totally believe you. I didn't think you weren't telling the truth. I just thought maybe you'd missed something, even though you got it all."

"That would have been a lot to miss," James told her.

"That's true," Kimama said. "But I just couldn't think of any other explanation. It didn't even occur to me that the library had gone all night unlocked." She looked at Sadie for confirmation. "I mean, can you imagine?"

"Well, it would be one very good explanation for how the other damage got done," Sadie said. But as she said it, her heart sank. As they'd been trying to figure out who might have done the damage to the instrument, or caused the later mischief among the boxes for the artifacts in the storage room, she'd been assuming that whoever it was, somebody in the library must have had the chance to see them.

But if the library had been standing open at night, all night, for days possibly, the list of possible suspects suddenly increased to include just about anyone in Silver Peak. As she stood looking down at the piles of cans, thinking there might be even more suspects now than there were of them, Kimama squared her shoulders and took a deep breath.

"This can't have been what you came in for, though," she said. "What brings you here? What can I do for you?"

"Well," Sadie said, "I'd just been doing a little bit of research into the Granby family tree, as you asked me to."

Kimama nodded.

"And I found something," Sadie said.

At this, Kimama's eyes widened hopefully. "What?" she said.

"Something I'm having trouble explaining," Sadie told her, and quickly related how her search for a connection to the Granby family tree had led her to the story of the little girl who had gone missing, Agatha.

"But you know how searches on the Internet go," Sadie said. "It's always too much information, or not enough of it, repeated over and over."

Kimama smiled wryly.

"So I thought I'd come here," Sadie said, "where we've got some real archives. And see if we had any better luck doing some old-fashioned research into the story of Agatha Barnhill."

"That sounds like exactly the kind of thing we'd like to do," Kimama said. "Some actual research. I'll take a look through a few of the local Silver Peak histories. James, would you like to help Sadie with the newspaper archives?"

"But what about all these cans?" James asked, struggling to his feet.

"They'll still be here when we're done," Kimama said. "And they'll be fine. That's the point of canned goods."

Sadie was glad to see Kimama's familiar grin appear as she made this joke. She'd seen too much worry and distraction on her face recently, ever since the instrument had been broken.

As Kimama headed toward the local history shelves, James came around from behind the counter with a shy smile, and Sadie trailed him over to the computer bank where the digitized versions of the *Silver Peak Sentinel* could be accessed.

"Can you remind me of the name again?" he asked, opening up a search box.

"Yes," Sadie said. "Thank you. It's Agatha Elizabeth Barnhill."

Even as she was speaking, James was already typing. He hit the Enter key, and several dozen articles popped up, all from around the time of the event that Sadie had been looking at the previous day. But where the Internet historians had been mostly patchily connected, and interrupted with big blocks of distracting text full of the authors' speculations, these were orderly and complete, so that they could get a very clear sense of the events, simply from reading the new reports that had come out each day.

The first article that mentioned Agatha carried a picture of her, and asked for help in locating her, as she had gone missing. It mentioned that her family was worried, and eager for any word. But perhaps because it had been written in haste, perhaps because of the time, or perhaps because Silver Peak was such a small town in those days, it didn't mention the names of her family, other than as Mr. and Mrs. Barnhill.

The next day, the paper started to fill with the rumors that had begun to swirl around the girl's disappearance. The community clearly had a deep suspicion of the trappers who still roamed the woods outside of town, but who hadn't yet seen fit to throw their lot in with the small band of settlers who clearly considered themselves more "civilized" than the men who still lived by their wits beyond the growing town. There hadn't been any particular sightings, as far as Sadie could tell, but suspicion fell on them nonetheless.

On the other hand, several people reported having seen a band of native people moving through the area in the days before Agatha's disappearance. The number of those reports only grew as the days passed and, to Sadie, they were relatively convincing. They weren't full of vague unease and unfounded suspicion like the charges leveled against the possible trappers. Instead, they described what sounded like basically the same band, again and again—thirty or so people, with groups of outriders or scouts who seemed mostly to appear in groups of two to three young men.

They hadn't come into town to trade, as many bands of natives apparently did. But they'd stayed in the area long enough for half a dozen witnesses to catch sight of them, and make basically similar reports of their activity—and the fact that they'd vanished at almost exactly the same time that Agatha did.

But here, their lack of knowledge about the people who lived around them left the people of Silver Peak at a disadvantage. They weren't able to accurately identify what group of people the band might have been part of, or how to find or negotiate with them again.

And as far as Sadie could tell, the reports of any romantic misadventure had purely been fabricated by an out-of-town paper that had caught wind of the story. At twelve, Agatha was old enough to believe that she might have fallen in love. But the odds of a child that young running off to try to start a new life with a sweetheart, especially one her own age, struck Sadie as too long to be believable.

Just as the town had been in the days after Agatha's disappearance, Sadie was riveted by the story, hoping with each new page to discover something that might lead her to the young girl's whereabouts—or simply announce her return, safe and sound. Almost breathlessly, she read the accounts of outsiders who rode into town to help—a federal marshal from Denver, a famous sharpshooter, a sheriff from a nearby town. But none of them had any more luck than Silver Peak's own law enforcement had.

And eventually, the reports came only every few days. Then every few weeks. Then every few months, simply announcing that there had been no further new developments, despite the letters they received asking for some, or alerting the town that the flashy big-city deputy had packed his bags and was on his way home.

Then nothing.

"So they never found her?" James asked.

17

"IT DOESN'T SEEM LIKE IT, ANYWAY," SADIE SAID.

"What do you think happened?" James asked, turning toward her.

"I don't think we know enough to guess at that," Sadie said. "Especially not from this distance."

"I don't see why everybody wanted to blame the natives," James said, and Sadie realized that for him, this story wasn't just about satisfying his curiosity. It was personal. It would have had a different feel to read the reports of local "savages" in the paper, if those people were your own ancestors, whom you knew to be something quite different.

"That's a very good question," Sadie said.

James leaned back in his chair, staring at the final results of the search.

"What about any other members of the Barnhill family?" Sadie asked. "Can we find any more information in the papers about what happened to them? Or about where she connects to the family tree?"

James typed a few keystrokes and a whole new screen of results flashed up. But there were no birth announcements for

Agatha or Anne, as Sadie had been hoping there might have been. And almost no record of Etta's grandmother Anne, either, until the announcement of her death.

"It's so strange," Sadie said. "The names are so similar, but we just can't make the connection back between Agatha and the Barnhill family. And *Anne* and *Agatha* are close enough to each other that I'd be tempted to think it was just a typographical error of some sort, except that the stories about Agatha ran for so long and so prominently in the Silver Peak papers. If there had been some mistake, surely somebody would have noticed the error at some point in the coverage of that story."

"It was a very big story," James agreed. "It would have been hard to miss."

Sadie leaned back in her seat beside him. As she did, she could see Kimama approaching out of the corner of her eye. When she turned her head to greet her, Kimama gave her a rueful smile and shook her head. "It looks like you two didn't have any better luck than I did," she said. "I'm afraid I couldn't find anything that would help us understand where Agatha fits into the Barnhill family. Although there were several articles on the disappearance, or as they characterized it, the kidnapping. All drawn from the *Sentinel* articles, which you've no doubt already read."

By now, Kimama was only a few steps away from them. But just before she reached them, she turned her head, glancing for a moment at the front door, where a man in a tasteful plaid trench coat was heading out. As he did, he turned his face to the side for a moment, to say good-bye to the clerk who was manning the desk.

And the instant he did, Kimama bolted after him.

The change in her trajectory was so abrupt, and so extreme, that both James and Sadie also leapt to their feet.

In a moment, they were chasing after Kimama, who had rushed to the door just in time to catch it before it swung shut behind the man in the trench coat.

When they reached her, she had already made it through the entry lobby where the book return and donation boxes stood, and was standing at the top of the library steps, scanning the entire area with a sharp eye.

"What is it?" Sadie asked, as she and James tumbled through the door behind Kimama onto the library steps.

"What's going on?" James asked. "Is everything all right?"

Kimama didn't take her eyes from the library's immediate surroundings to glance back at either of them, even for an instant.

"He was just here," she said. "And the door hadn't even shut when I caught it. He can't have gone far."

"Who?" James asked.

"The man from before," Kimama said. "Mr. Kilgore."

"The one who was here the day the instrument was damaged?" Sadie asked.

Kimama nodded. "And who was showing such a strange interest in the exhibit even before that," she said.

As she did, the engine of a car that was parked on a nearby curb purred to life.

Kimama started. "Is that him?" she said, bending over in hopes of catching a glimpse of the driver through one of the front windows. But for the moment, it was fruitless. Their elevation on the library steps meant that they were positioned so that they would have had to have X-ray vision to see through the roof of the car, and even then, at their angle, they only would have been able to see the back of his head.

The car pulled away from the curb, and into traffic, just as James sprinted down the steps after it.

"James!" Kimama said, coming down the steps after him. "Stop! Be careful!"

Heedless, James ran down the sidewalk to the vacant parking spot, crossed it in two bounds, then sprinted several yards down the empty street after the car. When it outpaced him, he jogged back to the library steps, where Kimama stood, hands on her hips.

"I want it to be very clear that that was in no way an official library assignment," she said. "In fact, I want to state clearly now that the library is highly displeased by your behavior as an intern."

James looked at the ground, abashed. "I just wanted to find out who it was," he said.

"I appreciate your dedication," Kimama said, slightly mollified. "But there is nothing in the library that is more important than your life. Or anyone's life. Under no circumstances do I ever want to see you putting yourself in harm's way for anything that has to do with this library, no matter how seemingly pressing, again. Do you understand?"

James nodded.

"All right," Kimama said, turning to lead them back up into the library.

"But don't you want to know what I found out?" James called from the foot of the steps.

18

"Found out?" Kimama repeated, turning around.

James gave a bashful nod. "I was trying to read the license plate," he said.

"Oh, James," Kimama said, her voice tired, "that's very sweet. But I doubt that the police are going to run a plate for us without evidence of a crime. So thank you, but..." She turned away again, heading up another few steps.

As she did, James came up after her, taking two steps at a bound with his athletic stride.

With a sigh, Sadie turned to follow the two of them.

"I understand all of that," James said. "But that's not all I saw."

"It's not?" Kimama said, stopping at the top of the steps, just outside the entrance to the library's outer lobby.

James shook his head.

"What else did you see?" Kimama asked quickly.

"There was a sticker on the back window," James said. "I couldn't read it, but I recognized the image, because I have a friend who goes there, and it looks just like his."

"Looks just like his what?" Kimama said, becoming almost impatient in her eagerness to hear the answer. "Where does your friend go?"

"It's a parking permit," James said. "For Blue Pine Community College."

"A permit?" Kimama repeated.

James nodded. "I don't think they give them to anyone who isn't part of the college, somehow," he said. "So maybe Mr. Kilgore has something to do with it."

Kimama snapped on her heel, and turned back to the library. Then she marched in, directly to the console of her own computer, behind the library's front desk.

"A Mr. Kilgore at Blue Pine Community College is a lot more searchable character than a Mr. Kilgore anywhere in Colorado. Or the whole United States," Sadie said.

Kimama nodded with determination. "That's exactly what I was thinking," she said, typing furiously.

From the other side of the counter, both Sadie and James watched her closely.

For a long instant, Kimama scanned through what must have been several pages of search returns. She clicked, then clicked again, navigating through pages. Then, suddenly, she drew in her breath. "That's him," she said. "I'd know him anywhere."

"Can I see?" James asked.

Kimama turned the screen of the computer around to show the photo of a man beside a biography of Chip Kilgore, who seemed to be a professor at Blue Pine Community College. The accompanying photograph was small, but in crisp focus.

"You're right," James agreed. "That's him."

Sadie scanned down the page, looking at the list of classes he taught, until her eye caught on another detail: his office hours. Calculating quickly, she realized that they were for this afternoon, just a few hours from now.

"That's today," she said.

"What?" Kimama said, looking back up at her.

"His office hours," Sadie said. "He might even be on his way to them right now."

Kimama scanned the page where Sadie had pointed. She shook her head.

"There's no way James or I could make that," she said. "It's not even just getting all these cans in order," she added, with a nod toward the still-unexplained bounty of the night's offerings from the good people of Silver Peak. "We're so close to the exhibit party now that there's just no time for anything else. If we spend all our work hours from now until the event, we'll still barely get it done."

"Oh, we'll get it done," James said, with youthful confidence.

Kimama smiled at his enthusiasm. "I'm sure we will," she said. "As long as we don't take any field trips to any professor's office hours in the next county." She looked back at the page again. "We'll just have to deal with it sometime after the exhibit," she said.

"Or," Sadie said, swinging her purse onto her shoulder, "I could go."

———

A few minutes later, she was tooling down the curves of one of Colorado's beautiful country roads, the last green grass of summer fading into the dormancy of winter, the next view always a slight surprise around the twisting corners and new vantage points that were constantly provided by the winding path of the road.

Lord, she prayed. *It seems like the more we try to learn about what's been going on at the library, the less we know.* At this, she gave a wry smile. Their situation this week, she realized, was actually a lot like life. She stared out at the road as it rolled away under the wheels of her car.

It was only a few more miles to the campus of Blue Pine Community College, where Sadie parked her car in front of what seemed to be one of the main academic buildings, and went in.

At the long desk just inside the door, she paused to talk with the receptionist, a pretty blonde woman in a green sweater who welcomed her with a cheerful "Hello!"

"Hello," Sadie responded.

"Can I help you with something?" the woman asked.

Sadie was surprised by her enthusiasm, but as she noticed all of the undergraduates shuffling along behind her, paying no attention to the receptionist at all, she realized she perhaps had a clue to the girl's desire to engage. It looked like she didn't get much foot traffic at all, and she was probably delighted to have a break in what might otherwise be a pretty boring day.

"I hope so," Sadie told her with a smile. "I'm looking for Professor Kilgore. Can you direct me to his office?"

"Sure," the girl said, pointing down the hall. "You're in luck. It's in this main building, down this main hall on the right. Number"—she checked a listing of names and numbers beside her phone, and looked up, her smile still bright—"113," she said.

Then she leaned forward confidentially. "You're lucky," she said. "If he was a biologist, you'd have to trek all the way across campus to the labs."

As the girl said this, Sadie realized she didn't even know what kind of professor Kilgore was. "And what," Sadie said, trying to keep her tone inquisitive but light, "does Professor Kilgore teach?"

The girl's expression clouded for a moment, as if she couldn't quite fathom why Sadie would be here to visit Professor Kilgore if she didn't even know what he taught. But any doubts she had on the matter were clearly overpowered by her eagerness to give the right answer.

"He's in the anthropology department," the girl said. "He's our assistant chair."

"Thank you so much," Sadie said quickly, before the girl could think of any questions to ask her. And she plunged into the stream of students who were moving up and down the hall, and followed it along with them to number 113.

To her relief, the door was propped partly open, enough so that she could see a single figure inside—along with the corner of the plaid trench coat she had just seen earlier that day, hanging from the back of the door. But the professor was alone, so she wouldn't have to wait for a student to leave in order to talk with him.

She raised her hand and knocked on the door.

Inside, a chair rattled across the floor. Then the door swung open and a kindly looking man with wire-rimmed glasses and a thick head of curly dark hair peered up at her.

"Hello?" he said. "Can I help you?"

Sadie stepped into the office and gestured to the chair, which was clearly there for visitors and students.

"Do you mind if I sit down?" she asked.

Still surprised, Professor Kilgore nodded, and gestured to the chair.

Sadie took a seat and smiled.

"Now," Professor Kilgore asked, "I'm sorry, but I'm afraid I don't recognize you from any of my classes. And I'm afraid that our classes have been in session long enough by this time in the term that I don't have an excuse. Are you one of our nontraditional students?"

Sadie laughed. She knew that people her age did sometimes return to college, and she'd actually considered taking a class or two herself. But she shook her head. "That's a lovely idea," she said. "But the last time I was on campus was over forty years ago."

Professor Kilgore nodded, taking that in. "Well then," he said, "what brings you here today?"

"I'm working with the Silver Peak Library," Sadie said.

"Oh?" Professor Kilgore responded, suddenly far more guarded than he had been when he offered her the seat.

Sadie nodded. "Yes," she said. "And I believe you're familiar with the exhibit on native artifacts that's going on there. The librarian has seen you there several times."

Professor Kilgore closed the book on his desk and leaned forward with an expression that seemed to Sadie to border on the defensive. "I'm sorry," he said. "Is the library in the habit of paying personal visits to all of its patrons at their own places of business?"

Sadie smiled, in an attempt to defuse the situation. "I know this is unusual," she said. "But we've had something unusual happen at the library."

Now Professor Kilgore's face filled with concern. "What's that?" he said. "Has something happened to the artifacts?"

The concern on his face was so genuine that Sadie decided to go ahead and tell him the story. His expression certainly didn't seem like the reaction of a man who would deliberately damage one of the priceless artifacts. And even if he had something to do with it, perhaps his further reactions would help her understand better what was going on.

"I'm afraid so," Sadie told him.

"Which one?" Professor Kilgore demanded. "What happened?"

Sadie leaned back, pleased that Kilgore had at least revealed that he was familiar enough with the exhibit to remember the various pieces. "You seem very familiar with the exhibit," she said. "That's actually why we were hoping to talk with you. We were looking for anything that was out of the ordinary during the time frame in which the instrument was damaged. Silver Peak is such a small town that the librarian and staff usually recognize most people who come in. They didn't recognize you. But they could see clearly that you had a very strong interest in the exhibit."

Professor Kilgore looked at her closely, as if measuring her up and making his own decision about her. Then he sat back in his own seat and grinned.

"I'm not sure I even want to know how you tracked me down to this office," he said, "if none of you recognized me."

"Well, you did share your name with one of our assistants," Sadie said. "And then he also saw the parking sticker indicating that you were somehow associated with this college."

Now Kilgore laughed out loud. "I'd like to have you along the next time I do fieldwork," he said. "It sounds like you don't miss a thing."

Sadie found herself liking this big man with the big laugh. But, she reminded herself, she still didn't have an explanation for why he had been lurking around the library. Or why he had been so unfriendly to Kimama when Kimama had tried to draw him out.

"So can you tell me about your interest in the exhibit?" Sadie asked.

At this, Kilgore's open expression did seem to stiffen a bit. "Oh," he said, "I've always been interested in native artifacts. It's part of my work."

"But you visited the Silver Peak Library several times," Sadie pressed. "Was there something especially interesting to you about this particular exhibit?"

"Professors become professors because they're interested in things that most other people don't find interesting," Kilgore said. "I'm afraid it's just a symptom of the profession."

But by now, Sadie was certain there was something he wasn't telling her. "I would have thought," she said, "if you were interested in the exhibit, that you would have been delighted to talk to its curator, Kimama. But her sense was that you were actually uneasy when she tried to welcome you to the library."

Kilgore sat back in his chair and stared at Sadie hard.

"And what is your involvement with all of this?" he asked. "Why didn't Kimama come herself, if she's so interested in the time I spent observing the exhibit?"

"I run an antique store in Silver Peak," Sadie said. "Kimama asked me to help her identify the piece that got broken. And now I'm trying to help her find out what happened to it."

"So you're somewhat of an expert yourself?" Kilgore asked.

"I'm not sure I'm an expert," Sadie said. "But I definitely care about things from the past, and what they mean. I want to see them preserved and cared for properly. To me, that's actually a lot more important than expertise."

To her surprise, Kilgore smiled. "It sounds like we have more in common than you might think," he said.

"Why do you say that?" Sadie asked.

"That's why I was at the library," Kilgore said. "To make sure the pieces were protected."

"But you don't have anything to do with the exhibit," Sadie said. "Do you?"

Kilgore laughed. "No," he said. "Not officially. But my area of study isn't just native artifacts. It's the way they're treated in the present day. Who owns them, or claims to own them. How they're treated. How they're presented to the world. I write about it. But I also try to do something about it."

"What do you do?" Sadie asked.

"I just keep my eye out," Kilgore said. "Any display of native artifacts that's within striking distance, I go and take a look at. I'm always checking to make sure that the items on display were well-sourced—not stolen or misused. And small places like the Silver Peak Library don't always have the resources to take care of artifacts in the way they ought to be treated, even if they are ethically sourced. So I also like to take a look to make sure that the history is being preserved in the best way possible. And if there are problems, I alert the proper authorities, and try to make sure there's some accountability as far as how we treat native objects, many of which have deep personal or sacred meaning to people who are still living today."

"Then why did you refuse to talk to Kimama?" Sadie asked. "I'm sure she would have loved to have had that conversation with you. And I suspect you can see for yourself what an extraordinary job she has done with the exhibit."

Kilgore nodded. "I could," he said. "She's obviously got a personal connection with the items, so she takes an extra degree of care, both in the ethics with which she collected the exhibit, and the presentation itself."

"Then why not just tell her that?" Sadie asked. "Why did you refuse to speak with her?"

Kilgore nodded, rubbing his jaw. "Well, you've just shown me how easy it is to compromise my anonymity. And I guess I'm going to just have to trust you not to spread the word of my private investigating on this topic around. But the fact that librarians and curators don't know that I do this work makes it much easier for me to do it. If they don't see me coming, they can't do slapdash efforts to cover up shoddy work—or prevent me from coming in at all."

"I see," Sadie said.

"But you didn't just come here because you were curious about my presence in the library," Kilgore said. "You mentioned that something else had happened." His eyes were full of concern. "Kimama had an extraordinary collection of pieces there. And I didn't notice any missing this morning. What has been going on?"

"First of all," Sadie said, "can you tell me where you were on this evening?" She tapped the calendar on his desk, indicating the night the instrument had been damaged.

"Sure," Kilgore said. "I was out of town. There was an academic forum in Denver that I attended. Had to give a paper.

There weren't a lot of people in the room, but I guess that's the nature of the beast."

Sadie sighed. If she grew more suspicious of him for any reason, she could always try to check that alibi. But for now, along with everything else he'd said, she had the sense that she could probably trust him.

"The piece that got damaged hadn't been put on display yet," Sadie explained. "Kimama had been trying to get the local owners to share it with the community for years, and they had finally agreed. But it was such an unusual piece that Kimama planned to unveil it at the exhibit celebration, later this week. She asked a local musician to take some time to learn to play it, and he'd been working with it for a few days..."

"When he damaged it?" Kilgore said, shaking his head. Sadie had listened patiently to his speeches about his passion for native artifacts. But she could see it evident now, in his eyes, which showed deep pain at the idea that one of the artifacts had been damaged. "That's so troubling. Did he just not understand its importance?"

"As far as we can tell, he did," Sadie said. "He and Kimama had a very strict protocol worked out, to ensure the safety of the instrument. She wouldn't even let him take it out of the library to practice."

"So what happened?" Kilgore asked.

"That's what we're trying to establish," Sadie told him. "We believe it happened at night, while the library was closed and the staff were gone. But we have no idea why anyone would have wanted to damage the instrument."

"Perhaps it has something to do with its history," Kilgore said. "Had you had much luck placing it, before the damage was done?"

Sadie shook her head. "I've done quite a bit of work on it, actually," she said. "But without getting many clear answers. I had Dr. Gramas over from Denver to take a look at it this week, but he wasn't able to come to any solid conclusions."

Kilgore nodded with a warm smile. "That's Gramas," he said. "He's a good social scientist. That means he won't tell you he knows the answer if he doesn't."

"I got that sense," Sadie said. "Although I wish he'd been able to tell us something more."

"I'm sure he did too," Kilgore said. "But sometimes the only honest thing to say is, 'I don't know.' And not enough experts do that, in my opinion."

"Maybe not," Sadie said.

"What about the family who had it in their possession?" Kilgore asked. "There must be some kind of family stories about how it came into their hands."

"That's exactly what I thought," Sadie said. "But the younger generation doesn't seem to know anything about it at all. And the older generation"—she thought back to her awkward visits with Beverly—"they've been very reluctant to talk about it."

"That's not unusual," Kilgore said. "Especially when there actually is a serious story there. One that might not cast the family in the best light if it was shared."

"And I did find one other thing, in my own research on the family," Sadie said. "Something that's been interesting to me—and frustrating."

"Oh?" Kilgore asked. "What's that?"

"In your research on the relations between natives and settlers in the area," Sadie asked, "have you become familiar with a story about a girl who disappeared around the same time a group of natives were seen in the area? The local papers were full of the suggestion that she'd been kidnapped."

Kilgore nodded. "Agatha Barnhill," he said. "Yes, she's actually an important figure. Her disappearance, and the rumor that it might have been an abduction, led to some pretty severe friction between native people and settlers. Her case led the government and army to take a harder line in conflicts with natives, whether they were suspected of having anything to do with her disappearance or not. Although it's not clear how concerned the lawmakers and military leaders were with Agatha herself, I think it's significant that they never mounted a big military effort to rescue her. They seemed much more interested in protecting the land that the settlers had claimed as their own. But that was a very big case at the time. It's impossible to study the history of the area without learning about it."

Sadie chuckled. "Well, I've studied the area's history quite a bit and hadn't heard about it until now."

He smiled. "Did she have a connection with the family who had the instrument?" he asked.

"Well, that's the strange part," Sadie said. "The Barnhill family married into the family that's now in possession of the instrument. But we haven't been able to find where Agatha Barnhill fits into that family tree, if she does. It was so early in the history of the town that the records are spotty, as is the newspaper reporting at the time."

Kilgore nodded. "Yes, papers of the day were often just a way to make a quick return on investment by throwing anything down on the page."

"And as far as I can tell from the articles in the *Silver Peak Sentinel*," Sadie said, "Agatha never returned to her family. So that still doesn't answer the question of how the instrument came to be in their hands."

Kilgore raised his eyebrows as if he had something to add.

"Do you know something I don't?" Sadie asked.

"Not necessarily," Kilgore said. "You're right, according to the official accounts at the time, and over the following decades, Agatha Barnhill never returned home. But you have to remember, out on the frontier, identity was a very fluid thing. People came out here because they wanted a chance to change who they'd been out East. So people tended to take each other at face value, and not ask too many questions about their backgrounds—so that nobody would ask too many questions about their own."

"Are you saying she might have returned under a different name?"

"I'm saying that the fact that her name never appeared again in the press or the historical records doesn't mean that she didn't live a long life," Kilgore said.

"With natives?" Sadie asked.

Kilgore shrugged and spread his hands to indicate that nobody could know for certain.

"Or with her own community," he said.

"Are you saying you think the rumors of abduction aren't true?" Sadie asked. "Do you think she was a runaway, perhaps? Or was somehow separated from her family involuntarily?"

"That's always possible," he said. "But I'm actually thinking of another story. One you wouldn't have found in issues of the *Silver*

Peak Sentinel. Or in the local history books. But I've just heard it in the course of my own research, several times."

"What's that?" Sadie asked.

"It's not a story that circulated among settlers, apparently," Kilgore said. "But the story of Agatha Barnhill was an important one in the native community, as well. As I was telling you, the rumor of her abduction led to suffering for the people in this area, and across Colorado."

"Yes," Sadie said. "I understand."

"Well, it's persisted until the present day. Many modern natives still have a memory of it. But when I've heard it mentioned, they mention something else, as well."

"What's that?" Sadie asked.

"That the girl was returned to her people."

Sadie's eyes widened. "What?" she said. "When?"

Kilgore shook his head. "That's all I've ever heard," he said. "I have asked, but it was so long ago that that seems to be all that remains of the story. At least among the people I've talked to. But I have talked with quite a few."

"But it was such a huge story when she vanished," Sadie said. "Wouldn't it have been an even bigger story if she came back? You'd think that would have filled up the papers in Silver Peak for weeks. Not to mention all the other places where it had also been news."

"I don't know," Kilgore said.

Sadie smiled. "Are you trying to prove to me you're a true scholar by saying that?" she asked.

Kilgore shook his head. "I didn't even think of that," he said. "But I'll take it as a compliment."

"I just can't understand why her family at least wouldn't have celebrated her return. And why she never seems to connect to the Barnhill family in any clear way, either before or after her disappearance."

"Like I said," Kilgore said, "I can't tell you that. But I can tell you that life was a lot more complicated than we sometimes imagine in the early days of white settlement in Colorado. And that, in my experience, the published history is never the whole story. There's always another part of the story, something that didn't get written down, or publicized.

"And often," Kilgore added, leaning back in his chair, "the history you have learned doesn't make sense until you hear about the history you haven't."

19

SLOWLY AND CAREFULLY, SADIE UNSCREWED THE CLAMPS THAT had been holding the face of the instrument to the back, which she had set there after gluing the two of them together the night before with an even bead of archival quality glue.

She pulled a nearby light closer and adjusted its neck so that she could get a better view of the face of the instrument, on which she had painstakingly glued the few splintered pieces back the day before, and the curve of the belly of the instrument.

She took a deep breath as the final clamp came loose and clattered onto the worktable in the back of the Antique Mine. Then she checked the wear marks on the wood of both pieces, where they had originally fit together.

The repair was almost invisible, even to her.

Sadie gave a sigh of relief and felt a strange tugging at her heart. She had been so concerned with getting things right that she had held down her emotions about the instrument. Now she felt a wave of gladness and satisfaction that the repair had been so successful. But along with it came something else—a sense of sadness that anyone would ever have done harm to such a beautiful instrument. And something even more than that—a deep sense of loss for the culture that had birthed the instrument, and how much of it could never be recovered, no matter how carefully anyone tried to repair it.

"How's it going, Grandma?" Theo asked, stepping into the back room.

"Well," Sadie said, stepping back, "I think I've done the best I can. It's just a matter of hearing from Spike about how he thinks it sounds, despite the repair job."

Theo peered down at her handiwork. "Wow," he said. "It looks really great to me. I can't even tell where it was cracked and split before. Good job, Grandma."

Sadie gave her grandson an affectionate peck on the cheek.

"I hope you're right," she said. "But in any case, I'm glad to hear you say it."

"Spike's actually out front right now talking with Alice," Theo said. "Do you want me to send him in?"

"That's perfect," Sadie said, holding back a knowing chuckle.

Soon Spike came into the back room, and gazed lovingly at the instrument. "So you think it's all fixed now, eh?" he asked. He let out a low whistle.

"Sadie," he said, "you did an amazing job. I can't even see where it was broken."

When he met her eyes, she thought they looked brighter than usual. Was it possible that those were tears?

"I never thought it could look this good again," he said. "I'm so glad to see it."

"I'm glad you think so," Sadie said.

"And just in time too," Spike said. "With the exhibit celebration tonight. Alice was just telling me she's planning on being there."

Alice had followed Spike into the back room and looked at her mother with a slightly amused but tolerant expression, the same kind she might have had on her face at the antics of a charming but somewhat dimwitted puppy.

But Spike was clearly overjoyed at the news.

"I've got the song I plan to sing all ready," he said. "I was going to try to write my own, you know, inspired by some of the reading I've been doing on native history. But in the end, James taught me a traditional song, and I think that's the right thing to play. It's just so beautiful that I can't think of doing it any other way. All I did was change the lyrics into English, so that most of the people here in Silver Peak can understand them. He's going to sing the first few verses in the original language. And then I'm going to sing the translation, and he may join in with me on some of them."

"That sounds wonderful," Sadie said. "I'm looking forward to it."

As he always did, Spike beamed at Alice, as if she was the one who had just spoken, instead of Sadie.

"And I'm so glad the instrument is fixed," he said. "I'd been practicing on one of my guitars, because we couldn't be sure how the repair was going to go, and the show must go on," he said with a slightly nervous laugh. "But this just feels right, getting to use the instrument. Actually, especially since it's been repaired. Of course, I'll be real careful with it. I mean, I always was. But I'm glad we won't be treating her like she's too delicate to get out into the world anymore. This old girl was born to sing. And I'm going to make sure she gets a chance to."

Sadie smiled. "It's interesting you say that," she said, "because I had a call with Dr. Gramas back in Denver earlier this morning."

"Is he the one who was trying to get a bead on where this instrument might have come from?" Spike asked.

Sadie nodded. "Yes," she said. "And he found something interesting. He'd taken some pictures of the instrument while he was here, and he was showing them around to some of his friends in the university, and the native community."

"And what'd they say?" Spike said. "Could they tell him anything?"

Sadie nodded. "Yes. One of his friends recognized this writing as a song," she said, tracing the delicate decorative lines of mysterious text that graced the face of the instrument, looping around it, crossing over itself, and connecting again in a series of wide loops.

"A song!" Spike said. "That's perfect! Do you know what song it is?"

"I don't know it myself, of course," Sadie said. "But I can put you in touch with the person who recognized it."

"Maybe they can teach it to me," Spike said, his eyes alight. "Wouldn't that be amazing? To play the song that's actually written on the instrument, *on* the instrument?"

Sadie smiled at his enthusiasm, and the play on words. "It would be amazing," she said.

"Well," Spike said, "I probably can't get in touch with them in time to learn the song for tonight. But did that guy up in Denver tell you anything about it at all? Do you know anything about what it might be about?"

"He did say that it was a love song," Sadie said. "And he said that's somewhat unusual. I guess many times any text that would be given such a privileged place would have been ceremonial, or political, instead: something to be used in religious ceremonies, or to praise a ruler, or prepare for a battle."

"A love song," Spike mused.

Sadie could tell that Alice could barely restrain herself from rolling her eyes. But still, she was sensitive to Spike's sincerity, and the fundamental sweetness and good nature of his crush on her. So she just gave him a quick smile back—not encouraging, but still polite.

"Well, that's real interesting," Spike said, trying not stammer. "That's something to think about. So it's an instrument devoted to love, huh?"

"I guess you could see it that way," Sadie said.

"Well, I'm not one of these experts from Denver," Spike said, "but I sure like thinking of it that way." He ran his hand very carefully across the face of the repaired instrument.

"Welcome back," he said. "We're going to take good care of you from now on. And I hope you're ready. Because you're going to do some singing tonight."

He glanced back at Alice, who by this time was reaching the end of her patience with his adoration, sweet as it might be.

"Well, since you've got such big plans for the evening," Sadie said, "we'd better let you get back with this as soon as possible."

With Spike trailing behind her, she lifted the case with the orange velvet lining up onto the worktable, and carefully cradled the repaired instrument back into its rightful place. Then she snapped the fasteners of the case shut, gave the hollow case a satisfied tap, and pushed it over to Spike, who retrieved it from the worktable very carefully, with a grateful nod.

"Thanks for this," he said. "I'm going to try to live up to all the work you've done, tonight."

"I'll look forward to that," Sadie said. "But I think it's more important to live up to the work of whoever made it in the first place."

Spike ducked his head in agreement. "Right you are, ma'am," he said. "As always. Well, I guess I'd better get out of your hair."

"It's always lovely to have you here," Sadie said, following him back onto the shop floor. "No trouble at all."

When they reached the front counter, where Alice sat, again perusing her book, Spike drifted in her direction and then stopped directly before her as if drawn by a magnetic field. But when she looked up and gave him a friendly smile, he didn't seem to be able to remember anything about what he had meant to say.

"Hey," he said, as if he'd just walked into the store for the first time.

"Hey," Alice said. Sadie could see that she was struggling to contain her amusement, but she did a good job of it. Spike didn't have any sense at all that she was making fun of him—which she wasn't. But even Sadie had to admit that his crush on Alice did have comical qualities.

"Good book?" Spike asked.

Alice nodded, and threw him a bone by turning over the spine so that he could see what it was: *The Blue Flower* by Penelope Fitzgerald.

"Penelope Fitzgerald," Spike said, trying to nod sagely, as if he had any idea who she was. "She must be F. Scott Fitzgerald's little sister, right?"

Alice smiled, and Spike's face brightened with delight.

Then Alice shook her head. "No relation," she said. "Unless it was very far back in old Ireland. Penelope Fitzgerald was writing at the end of the 1900s, not the beginning."

"I never heard of her before," Spike admitted, as if Alice hadn't been able to figure this out until then.

"You're not alone," Alice said. "People are still learning who she is. But she's wonderful. She didn't start writing until she was well over sixty years old. In fact, she wrote her first book for her husband, as she was nursing him through his final illness. But then, she wrote book after book. Four of them were contenders for the biggest literary prize in England. One of them won it."

"That's a great story," Spike said enthusiastically. "It's never too late, is it?"

Alice smiled and shook her head. "I guess not," she said. "I mean, look at what Mom's done with this shop. She opened it right around the same time Penelope Fitzgerald started writing books."

"So I should be winning some kind of big prize any moment," Sadie joked. "Is that what you're trying to tell me?"

Alice gave her mom a wry look, but as usual, Spike couldn't bring himself to have eyes for anyone but her.

"So," he said, "what does she write about?"

"That's what's so amazing about her," Alice said, showing genuine enthusiasm for the first time in the conversation. Sadly for poor Spike, it wasn't enthusiasm for him, but for Penelope Fitzgerald. "She writes about all kinds of things. The reviewers are always dazzled that this little English housewife could write about such a broad range of themes. One of them is about a family living on a houseboat on the Thames."

"Well, that sounds like it's at least pretty close to home," Sadie said.

"Yes," Alice said. "And one of them is about radio operators during World War II. And there's one about a family of British expatriates living in Russia. And one about a woman who tries to start a bookstore in a haunted shop in a small country town."

"She does seem like she was kind of—all over the place," Spike said, still trying gamely to keep up. He nodded at the book in Alice's hands.

"What's that one about?" he asked.

Alice looked down at the cover, as if she'd forgotten all about it. "Oh," she said, "this one is about one of Germany's most famous poets."

Spike raised his eyebrows, blanching a bit at this description. "Well," he said, "that may be a bit too high-flown for me."

Alice shook her head, unable to believe that anyone wouldn't enjoy the book every bit as much as she did, including Spike, whom Sadie had to admit, did seem like an unlikely fan for a German romantic poet. "Oh no," she said. "Really it's a kind of love story. It's very simple...," she said. Then she thought for a minute, and smiled. "Except for the ways that it's actually complex."

Spike grinned, with some ground now to stand on in the conversation. "It seems like you've pretty much summed up most love stories," he said.

"Maybe I have," Alice said.

At this, Spike hiked the instrument case in the air, like a kid showing off the treasure he'd just dragged home from school. "Well," he said, "I guess I'd better get back over to the library. I need to get reacquainted with this old friend before the show tonight."

"Okay," Alice said, already looking back down at the next page. "See you there."

"See you there!" Spike repeated, his enthusiasm evident.

Sadie shook her head as he went through the door.

"Well," Sadie said, "I'm going to go and see about cleaning up the back room."

"I'll hold down the fort," Alice said.

"Whatever happens," Sadie told her. "I'm in earshot."

She threaded her way back through the maze of displays, which were still enough to catch her fancy and make her stop, even though, for the most part, she was the one who had created them—or at least authorized them. But she was glad that having the store was still a delight, and not just a job. At least most days.

After lingering for a minute by a silver tray displaying a set of beautifully hand-embroidered hankies, one for every month of the year, with corresponding foliage—evergreen for Christmas, violets for April, sunflowers in the fall—she stepped back into the back room.

For a few minutes, she puttered, cleaning up the dust and fragments from her repair of the instrument, reshelving the glue, and stashing the clamps in one of the special drawers where she kept them.

Then she picked up the piece of paper on which she'd taken notes when Dr. Gramas had called her back with his further research on the instrument. It contained all the information she'd just told Spike. But her eye was also drawn to something else.

Along the side, she'd doodled a list of items she wanted to ask him about. All of them were crossed off, except for the letters *AEBT* at the bottom. That was her note to herself, to ask him if any of his colleagues had offered him any explanation, or any hint at all as to what they might mean.

All of her other questions had been checked off with little *x*'s, meaning that Dr. Gramas had given her an answer. But *AEBT* had not. Instead, she had drawn a circle around it, with several question marks below it, to indicate that, even after showing his photographs of the instrument to multiple experts, and discovering the meaning of the decorative work depicting the native song, Dr. Gramas still had no idea what *AEBT* might stand for.

But perhaps because the letters were so starkly outlined on the otherwise fully scribbled-over page, or perhaps because of all the research she had done for herself since the last time she saw Dr. Gramas, something stood out to Sadie this time when she looked at the letters now: *AEB*.

They were the initials, Sadie realized, of the Granby grandmother whose family the instrument had come down through, Anne Elizabeth Barnhill. And also of the mysterious girl who had disappeared generations before this one, Agatha.

An instant later, Sadie had her keys in her hand, and was sailing back out the workroom door, heading through the shop, out to the street.

Beverly Granby might have claimed not to recognize the letters the first time Sadie tried to ask her about them.

But now Sadie could point out that they bore an uncanny resemblance to Beverly's own family history.

What would Beverly have to say in response to that?

20

SADIE HURRIED DOWN THE STREET, HEADING FOR HER CAR, which, due to the abundant street parking in Silver Peak, especially in the early morning hours when she usually got to the shop, was parked only a few spaces away.

But just before she reached it, something across the street caught her eye.

A man was walking down the opposite sidewalk, carrying a bulky object wrapped in paper. He would have been remarkable if only for walking down the street with such a big package—it was every bit as large as his own torso, and he was a big man and relatively powerfully built.

But it caught Sadie's eye in particular because the wrapping was very similar to the simple but effective paper-wrapping favored by many antique hounds, including herself. You could never build just the right box for all the odd-size objects that flowed through an antique shop, or through a booth at an antique market. But you could wrap almost anything up within an inch of its life, if you just had enough paper. And the paper was surprisingly protective, even for very delicate objects. So stacks of newspaper, or big, cheap craft rolls, were an integral part of most antique dealers' lives.

Sadie had always taken a special kind of delight in the way things changed when they were swaddled in paper: A vase could begin to look like a rotund man; a long, skinny package could be a pool cue or a lampstand. And when packages came to her wrapped in paper, she loved cutting them open to reveal what was inside. But even more than that, she loved the few minutes that she got to stand looking at the new item as it was still wrapped in paper, and trying to guess what it might be from the strange shape. She was almost always wrong, but she didn't mind. It wasn't about being right. It was about the pleasure of pretending that the package on the table in front of her might be anything at all, from a Russian samovar to a magic lantern.

At first, that was all she was doing—trying to get a good look at the package in the man's arms, so that she could play a private version of "guess the object," even if she would never get close enough to it to have a real answer.

But then, as she wondered about whether it might be some kind of large kitchen item, or perhaps even an instrument, she finally caught sight of the face of the man.

It was Steven, Spike's friend.

"What in the world...?" Sadie said to herself.

Then, checking traffic both ways, she darted across the street, and planted herself squarely in Steven's path.

He was in such a hurry to get to wherever he was going with his big package that at first he didn't even seem to recognize her.

So she gave him a bit of help. "Steven!" she exclaimed. "It's good to see you. How are you doing today?"

"Oh," Steven said with a hurried smile. "Mrs. Speers. I'm sorry, I didn't see you at first. It's good to see you too."

He was obviously hoping to just breeze past her, on his own way, but she continued the conversation with a bright smile.

"Now, what have you got there?" she asked. "From the looks of it, it would have to be a very big piece of jewelry."

Steven looked more than a little uneasy at this line of questioning. "Oh no," he said, "you're right about that. It's a little big for a piece of jewelry."

But he hadn't bothered to tell her what it actually was, Sadie noted. Because he seemed so uncomfortable, she decided to try to lighten things up with a joke.

"And I can't believe you've come up with a gemstone that big," Sadie said. "Or if you have, I'd be very impressed that you're carrying it down the street."

Steven seemed to try to humor her by bobbling the package in his arms as if it were a baby he was trying to amuse. From the way he did it, she could see clearly that it was quite light.

"Oh no," Steven said, "this isn't too bad. But you're right, a gem this size…" He let out a low whistle, then made another attempt to be on his way.

But as he did, Sadie caught sight of a part of the object that hadn't been covered by the paper wrapping. And when she did, she caught her breath. She couldn't make out what the object was from the small glimpse she had through a poorly taped fold of paper. But she could clearly see something that had the characteristic markings of many of the native artifacts Kimama had on display over at the library. Sadie wasn't expert enough to identify which tribe either. But she knew enough about antiques to see from the wear and coloration that it was something old. And that it wasn't from the tradition of Western antiques that she knew best, but from a completely different culture.

"Steven," she said, arresting him in his tracks with her biggest smile. "You're not going to leave me wondering like this, are you? 'Fess up! What's in the package?"

At this, Steven's eyes darted around the street, almost as if he expected a SWAT team to rise up from behind the rows of automobiles that lined the sleepy Silver Peak street. But when that didn't happen, he still didn't look relieved. He met Sadie's eyes again, seemingly stymied by what answer to give her, looked up at the sky, and then glanced at the ground.

"It's just something I've got to take care of," he said. "I'm sorry, I'm running a little late. Excuse me."

With that, he finally did break free of their conversation, and walked quickly up to the next corner, where he crossed the street, then disappeared between the library and the Bless Our Souls shop.

Sadie was after him like a flash. But instead of following him along the side of the street he had taken, she crossed back immediately. When she got to the corner, she paused and peered around it, catching sight of him just as he ducked into the alleyway that led to the tiny delivery bay for Bless Our Souls.

Trying to keep her footsteps quiet, Sadie followed him.

Before she even reached the alley, she could hear the sound of a car door opening and closing, and then what sounded like the popping of a trunk. When she got to the mouth of the alley, she continued to do her best to stay hidden, taking a glance around the corner without showing her whole form.

But by the time she got that close to him, Steven had apparently completely forgotten about her. He was leaning over the trunk of the car, carefully depositing his giant package into it.

Sadie still couldn't make out with any certainty what exactly was in that package. But she could clearly see something else: The trunk was stuffed to the gills with native artifacts. There were so many that it was hard to make out any one thing, but there were items of regalia, drums, even what seemed to be a small but beautifully wrought footstool.

Then Steven straightened, the new package in place, and slammed the trunk closed. He glanced to one side, and Sadie darted back around the corner just as he was about to glance her way. An instant later, she could hear the car starting.

Now it was her turn to hurry. But she made it up the block, and around the corner on to the main street, before he had a chance to pull out of the alley, and see her.

21

As she drove over to Beverly Granby's yet again, Sadie pondered what her strange encounter with Steven could possibly have meant. He had told her and Roz that he had a deep affection for native cultures, so it wasn't a complete surprise that he might collect some artifacts himself. But why would he have so many, especially at a time when his family was clearly strapped for cash? If they were part of a personal collection that he was proud of, why had he not lent any of them to the library, for the citywide exhibit? And most important, if there was some simple, aboveboard explanation for all of this, why had he been so strangely evasive with Sadie?

Sadie felt worried. The beautiful artifacts didn't belong in the back of somebody's car. They belonged on display for everyone to see, or with their own people. But she had a sickening feeling that she had just seen the fate of all too many native artifacts—that the ones Steven had driven away with in the back of his car were not the only native treasures that were too far from where they belonged.

And what did all of this have to do with the instrument? Spike hadn't told her anything about Steven having a collection of artifacts. And he'd been eager to tell her everything he knew. So there was a good chance that Steven hadn't mentioned anything about it to him. Was it possible after all that Steven had been hoping to add the instrument to his collection? That somehow he had made an attempt to steal it, but accidentally damaged it in the process? Or, she wondered, thinking about the second break-in at the library, was he even interested in the instrument? Or had he been "casing" the library, on the trail of one of the other artifacts that Kimama had collected for the exhibit?

Sadie pulled up to the curb of Beverly Granby's house again, her head full of questions and half answers.

To still them, she took a deep breath and prayed for guidance. She glanced up at the house, where she knew she would be less than welcome. She took a deep breath, got out of the car, and walked, almost reluctantly, up the trim front way, to the familiar red door.

She raised her hand to knock with a bit of trepidation, and then steeled herself to give her best smile, no matter what expression Beverly was wearing when she answered the door.

But to her surprise, it wasn't Beverly who answered.

"I'm sorry," Sadie blurted out to the pert elderly woman who stood within, wearing a blue chambray shirt and jeans. "I'm looking for Beverly."

"Well, I'm not sure you have anything to apologize for," the woman said, with a twinkle in her eye. "We'll have to get to know each other a little bit better before we get to all that."

Sadie grinned, disarmed immediately by her humor. "I'm Sadie," she said. "It's nice to meet you."

"I'm Etta," the woman said, sticking out her hand. "Beverly's mom. I'm afraid Beverly's not home right now. You just caught me as I'd stopped off to deliver her some Love Spell Cookies. I'm taking a baking class at our senior center this fall. I thought I was a pretty good baker, but some of the things they come up with—I tell you." She shook her head and laughed. "But I made Beverly promise before I signed up that she'd eat at least half of every batch of baked goods I made. Because I need to stay in shape for my water aerobics class too, you know." She winked. "I wish I could help you."

"Well," Sadie said, "maybe you can. I've actually been talking with Beverly a bit about your family history."

"Well, we certainly have one, don't we?" Etta said, with a wry look. "I never knew exactly what to think about all my august forebears. As far as I could tell, it didn't seem to do me much good that they'd gotten up to so many big schemes back in the day. It only seemed to make people expect more out of me. I guess maybe that's how I got the way I am. I always like to give them something they don't expect. But come in, come in. I'd be glad to tell you anything I can about it. And I've still got a few hours before I need to be over at the indoor pool."

"Thank you so much," Sadie said, following Etta's careful steps to the pretty chintz sitting room where she had visited with Beverly on her earlier visits.

When they were both seated in the comfortable chairs, Etta leaned forward. "Now," she said, "you'll have to tell me what you're interested in, exactly. And please don't ask me to tell you why my ancestor set up camp outside of town instead of just getting one of these nice city lots like we've got here now. I never could abide camping myself, even in the heart of summer. Whatever it was that convinced that man the wilderness was the best home for his family, even in the dead of winter, didn't transfer in my genetics, I can tell you that."

"Well, you certainly know your family history," Sadie said with a smile.

Etta rolled her eyes with her own good-natured smile. "In the Granby family, you can't get away without learning it," she said. "Believe me. Sometimes I would have liked to get away from all those distinguished ancestors. You know?"

"Well," Sadie said, "I'm not sure how distinguished my ancestors are."

"You see," Etta said, "that's exactly the kind of thing I wanted to be able to say. I mean, this is the Wild West, isn't it? People came out here to get away from all that respectability out East. And it's not just the West. It's America, isn't it? People coming over here to try to start a new life, beyond all the expectations about who a person had to be back in Europe."

Sadie nodded.

Etta took a deep breath. "But not my family," she said wryly. "Everyone else seemed to have a flimflam man or a disreputable trapper somewhere in their background. Or maybe they just didn't know much about their family, because they hadn't done much—except for survive out here, which I always thought was a pretty big accomplishment. But no! My family had to get respectable from day one. Starting mills. Building the town. They might let in a married-on from a family that lived in some crazy camp outside town. But they weren't going to move the family out there themselves. No sirree."

"Well," Sadie said with a grin, "they did have you. It sounds like you definitely have your own point of view."

Etta tilted her head. "You do have a point there," she said. "Now, what can I help you with? And how did you get interested in the Granby family history? You're not a relation of ours, are you?"

Sadie shook her head. "Not that I know of," she said. "Although that would be a pleasant surprise. No, I'm working with the library."

"The library?" she said. "Don't tell me they're writing another book about us. I swear, I know we helped to build the town of Silver Peak, but it seems like every other year, there's somebody else knocking on the door, wanting me to rehash the facts of yet another one of these old stories."

"I did see your family included in several of the local histories," Sadie said. "But that's not actually what I'm interested in myself. I've been working with Kimama, the head librarian there, on the exhibit of native artifacts that she puts on every year around the Thanksgiving holiday."

At the mention of this, Sadie thought she saw a strange glow in Etta's eye. But in response, Etta was uncharacteristically silent. So Sadie went on with her explanation.

"Candace, your granddaughter, was generous enough to lend an item to the exhibit this year. And Kimama asked me to do some research on it."

"Oh?" Etta said, her curiosity evident. "What item is that?"

Sadie's eyebrows leapt in surprise that Etta wouldn't be able simply to guess. Did she not know that the family treasure had been scheduled to go on display down at the library? But Candace had put it on loan without Beverly's permission. So there was no reason to believe that she would have told Etta either. But still, why would Beverly not have mentioned it to Etta once she found out? Sadie thought back on Beverly's impassioned charge not to talk with her mother about the instrument. What was behind it? Was she trying to protect Etta from something? Or to protect someone—or something—else?

"A beautiful instrument," Sadie said. "With some lovely designs and writing on its face. You must know it."

Etta's face broke into a smile. "Oh," she said, "I do. I hadn't realized that Candace was putting it on display. But that's wonderful. I'm so glad everyone is going to have a chance to see it."

This was a very different reaction from the one Beverly had had to the news, Sadie noted.

"Neither Beverly nor Candace seemed to know much about how it came into the family," Sadie said. "So I've been doing some research of my own. And one of the experts was able to identify the writing on the face of the instrument as a song. Apparently it's a kind of love song, which I'm told was actually somewhat unusual for the time. And the instrument itself is unusual, as well. It's not like anything else that was commonly used by native people in this area."

Etta nodded. "So you're curious about the instrument?" she said.

Sadie nodded.

As she did, the front door swung open. Someone stepped inside, and then there was the rattle of keys as they fell into some kind of dish in the front hall.

"Hello, honey!" Etta called out. "We're in here."

"Hey, Mom!" Beverly called back from the next room. "I didn't expect to find you still here. And who..."

She stepped into the sitting room, and got the answer to her question about who the mystery visitor was, before she even finished asking the question. Her reaction to Sadie's presence was quick, and unmistakable. Her eyes narrowed, and her lips pursed.

"This is Sadie," Etta said. "She's here with some questions about our old instrument. Candace has loaned it to the library for some kind of exhibit. And all kinds of exciting experts have been looking at it. It appears we've had something quite special on our hands."

"She's been here before," Beverly said, her words clipped and unfriendly. "In fact, I think I recall telling you that we weren't interested in answering any more of your questions."

But Sadie wasn't about to lose her chance. Beverly was already upset. There was nothing she could do about that. But she might be able to learn something else now, if she asked the right questions.

"It's just that I noticed something else in my research on the family, and the instrument," Sadie said. "Something I wanted to share with you, to get your perspective."

"Oh?" Etta said, leaning forward, her keen eyes full of interest. "And what is that?"

"Well," Sadie said, "I talked with Beverly earlier this week about some writing we found inside the instrument."

"The song you were talking about?" Etta inquired.

Sadie shook her head. "No," she said. "This was different. It wasn't on the face of the instrument, but the interior. And it was in the letters of the standard English alphabet."

"What did it say?" Etta asked.

"It wasn't a word," Sadie said. "Not that we could identify. But the letters were clear."

"What were they?" Etta pressed.

"AEBT," Sadie said. "Maybe you'd even seen it yourself, before."

Etta leaned back in her chair thoughtfully. "I don't know that I had," she said.

"Well, I thought perhaps the family would have some insight into their meaning," Sadie said, glancing at Beverly, whose face was still unwelcoming, darkened with anger. "She didn't see any immediate connection. But when I took a little closer look at your family history, I think I may have found one."

"Oh, really?" Etta asked. "What's that?"

"Well, the first three letters are AEB," Sadie said. "Those are the initials of one of your ancestors, if I'm reading the local histories correctly. Anne Elizabeth Barnhill."

"My grandmother," Etta said, softly.

Sadie nodded. "I wasn't sure about that," she said. *But that would make sense, based on the dates,* Sadie thought. "Did you know her well?" she asked.

Etta smiled. "My dad always said I could get to know her just by looking in the mirror. He always said I was the spitting image of her. But she didn't live long enough for me to know her very well. I remember a few things about her. There was a song she used to sing to me, or at least my dad told me she did. But I'm not sure if I learned it from her or from him. She died when I was just three years old. With memories that far back, I'm sure you know how it is. Especially once you get to be my age," she said with a laugh. "It's hard to tell what you remember, and what you've just been told."

"I know exactly what you're talking about," Sadie said.

"I still don't see any connection," Beverly snapped. "Those letters could mean anything. And what about the last one, the T?

You have to drop it to make any connection with our family. And even then, the connection still isn't clear. How does that prove that Mom's grandmother had anything to do with the instrument? It seems very much to me like you're reaching."

As she glanced over at her mother, Sadie thought she saw worry in her eyes, but she still couldn't tell if Beverly's concern was for her mother, or someone else, even herself.

"There is one other thing," Sadie said.

"What's that?" Etta asked. She seemed completely rapt in the conversation, to the point that she barely seemed to have noticed her own daughter's significant discomfort.

Sadie glanced from one of them to the other. She didn't want to cause any trouble within the family. But she also wanted to get to the truth about what had happened to the instrument—and what was going on at the library.

"They're also the initials of a girl who disappeared from Silver Peak. And who shares one of your family names. Agatha Elizabeth Barnhill. I haven't been able to establish whether she was a family member of yours or not. But—"

"Well, there you have it," Beverly said. "Yet again, nothing but the most tenuous connection. Barnhill is a common name. You said it yourself. You can't find any connection. And that's because," she said, raising her chin defiantly, "there isn't one."

"How did she disappear?" Etta asked quietly.

"Well," Sadie said, "there are a number of theories about that. She may have been a runaway. The surrounding areas at the time were wild enough that she could have wandered off and been lost in the mountains without being found. But there were also reports that a group of native people had been in the area where she was last seen, and left the area shortly after her disappearance from town. In any case, she was never seen again."

"Are you suggesting that one of our family members was kidnapped by Indians?" Beverly said, incredulous. "And that somehow that never came down in our own family history? I'm sorry," she said. "This is really too much. I didn't want to be forced to do this, but I'm going to have to ask you to leave."

With a sigh, Sadie rose to go. But as she did, Etta put her hand on her sleeve.

"It's true," she said.

"What?" Beverly said, her head swiveling toward her mother.

"It's true," Etta repeated, a bit more distinctly. "She was taken by a tribe. But it's not true that she was never seen again."

"It's not?" Sadie asked.

Etta shook her head. "She did come back home," she said.

22

FINALLY, BEVERLY SANK DOWN INTO A CHAIR BESIDE HER mother, her eyes wide with shock.

"Mother," she said. "What are you talking about?"

"I'm talking about my grandmother," Etta said.

"Grandma Anne?" Beverly said. "What does she have to do with this?"

"She's the little girl who was taken from Silver Peak," Etta said.

"What?" Beverly breathed. Suddenly, relief flooded into her face. "So that explains it."

"Explains what?" Etta asked.

"I got curious about the instrument, once," Beverly said. "And so I asked Dad about it. But he told me never to ask about it again. He said you might get very upset if I did. That's why I didn't want Sadie coming around, trying to introduce all these rumors. I was afraid they might upset you."

Etta smiled. "Your father," she said with a fond smile. "He was always trying to protect me. And he was right. These facts might have upset some people in Silver Peak. In fact, they might have upset your father's family so much he might not have married me. That's why we decided to keep it a secret from them."

"Keep what a secret?" Beverly asked.

"The fact that your great-great-grandfather was a tribal chief," Etta told her.

Beverly leaned back in her chair, her animosity toward Sadie gone, and her eyes filled with wonder. "How in the world?" she asked.

Etta took her hand, and Beverly's own fingers closed around it. "I'm so sorry to have kept this a secret from you," she said. "I often thought about telling you. Especially when you were so curious about the instrument, as a young girl."

"It was the only thing you ever refused to talk with me about," Beverly said. "You kept telling me you didn't know much about it, but I knew that couldn't be true. You and Grandad were so close. So I got the idea that something must be wrong about it. And as I got older, I began to understand a little more about the history of native people in this area. And I started to be afraid of what we might have had to do with it."

"There were some terrible things that happened to native people in Colorado," Etta said. "But this was more complicated than that."

"What happened?" Beverly asked.

"Well," Etta said, "this is how Daddy told it to me. I guess his mother, Agatha Barnhill, loved to explore the land outside town. She was a real tomboy I guess, climbing trees and wading through rivers, but also picking up stones and flowers to take home to her mother. And one day, when she was out, she crossed paths with a group of natives."

"And they kidnapped her?" Beverly asked, her face drawn with horror.

"That's one way to put it," Etta said. "And she did fight. And make several attempts to escape. But they were nomadic, and she quickly realized that they had traveled so far from anything she recognized that she would have a very hard time making her way back alone. And they were also kind to her. They needed more people, because their numbers were dwindling. So they made her work hard, but not harder than they did themselves. And there were things she loved about her life with them.

"Remember, she was very young, only twelve, so she still had a lot to learn about the world. And there weren't as many opportunities on the frontier, if you were a girl. But the native people had different ideas about what women could do. They had more freedom than Agatha had in Silver Peak. And they had a bigger say in the decisions in the community.

"So pretty soon, she had her own place in the tribe. And as she grew up, one of the tribal leaders took her as his wife, and she had his child."

"Your father?" Beverly asked.

Etta shook her head. "No," she said. "He was born a few years later. But by that time, the people Agatha was with had been squeezed by settlers and hunted by the army almost out of existence. Her husband did everything he could to keep his people safe and well-fed, but it was getting harder and harder. And then, one winter, a raiding party fell on to their camp. It was a peaceful camp, but the soldiers didn't seem to know that. They only spared Agatha because they recognized her as white by her blue eyes and blonde hair. So while they killed or ran off everybody else, they took her and her son captive."

"Her son?" Beverly said. "Didn't you say she had two sons?"

"I never knew what happened to the other one," Etta said. "He may have died in the raid. Or of some childhood illness."

"That's awful," Beverly said.

Etta nodded.

"So what happened to her?" Beverly said. "After the soldiers captured her?"

"She didn't know if her husband was still alive or not," Etta said. "And so she tried every way she knew how to escape. But then the soldiers told her that her husband was dead. She didn't believe them until they brought her an instrument that they had found in his tent. She recognized it right away. And she knew, if he was alive, that he would never have given it up."

"How?" Beverly said.

"Because he made it for her," Etta said. "She'd always loved music, and she was lonely for the mandolin and piano she'd had as a young girl from an up-and-coming family in Silver Peak. She didn't know what to do with the drums and the flutes that her tribe was used to using. So her husband told her he would make her something just for her. He'd seen cowboys with parlor guitars and other stringed instruments. So he built her one himself, from memory. With a song that he wrote just for her painted on the front of it...and her initials written inside."

"Agatha Elizabeth Barnhill...?" Beverly began.

"Tama," Etta said. "The name of her husband."

"AEBT," Sadie said softly.

"It was a wedding gift," Etta said.

"Why didn't you ever tell me before?" Beverly asked.

Etta sighed. "Well, it's a serious thing when your father makes you promise never to tell a secret," she said. "Believe me, I wanted to tell you. But I didn't want to break my promise to Papa. And it's not an easy story to tell. Times are different now, I know. And I wish Papa had lived to see a time when he could have known his grandchildren were proud to know about his background. But I'd kept the secret for so long, I guess I just got used to keeping it. It seemed like there was never just the right moment."

"I'm so glad you told me," Beverly breathed, reaching over to squeeze her mom's hand. "And I'm so glad you're not upset."

She turned to Sadie. "And I'm so sorry for the way I've treated you," she said. "I hope you can understand. I was afraid you were getting close to a story that would be very upsetting for Mom. And I wanted to protect her from anything I can."

"Oh, I can protect myself," Etta said, patting her hand. "I might even still be able to protect you from a thing or two."

Beverly smiled at her and gave her a kiss on the cheek.

"So," she said, sitting back in her own seat and beginning to put back together the pieces of her upended family history. "Agatha's baby was your father?"

Etta nodded. "That's right," she said.

"So what did he tell you about her?" Beverly said, learning forward to listen.

Etta took a deep breath. "Not very much," she said. "That's part of what's so sad about the story. She didn't live long after the soldiers brought her back to town. Of course, the family recognized her, and they were overjoyed to have her back. But she had been gone for over ten years. She had a whole other life, and a whole family of her own. She'd just lost it in a devastating way, so she was dealing with terrible grief and sorrow. And life back in town was very, very strange compared to what she had grown used to. She didn't like the clothes she was expected to wear. She missed her friends, and her husband."

"It sounds awful," Beverly said.

"I think it must have been," Etta said. "And perhaps maybe she suffered some kind of shock or injury in the attack on her camp. Because she died less than a year after she returned to Silver Peak."

Beverly shook her head.

"I'm curious about something," Sadie asked. She had been waiting to allow Beverly and Etta to share the family story, because it seemed like such an important moment for them. But she was also thinking about all the research she had done on the family. And a few things still hadn't been explained.

"What's that, dear?" Etta asked, turning to her.

"It was such a huge case when Agatha disappeared," Sadie said. "And as you said, I imagine the family was overjoyed when she returned home. So why didn't they tell anyone?"

When Sadie asked the question, Beverly turned to her mother as well, curiosity in her own eyes.

"Because of Papa," Etta said.

"Her son," Beverly said.

"That's right." Etta nodded. "She didn't just come home. She came home with a baby. A baby with a native father. At a time when there was extreme tension between settlers and natives. As Papa told me, they decided to keep her identity a secret to protect him. So when she came home, they changed her name slightly."

"To Anne," Sadie said.

"Yes. They told the people in town that she was a cousin, named Anne. It might have gotten quite complicated if she had survived long enough to become part of the social life in Silver

Peak. But she wasn't able to do that before she passed away. And when she passed away, the family simply adopted Papa as their own grandson."

"Which he was," Beverly said.

"Yes," Etta said.

"It's such an amazing story," Beverly said.

"I'm sorry I didn't tell you before," Etta told her.

"I understand why you didn't," Beverly said. "But I'm glad you have now."

She gave her mother a long hug, then pulled away.

"And I guess I have a lot to learn, now, about my own heritage."

"I guess so!" Etta said, her eyes beginning to twinkle. "You know, I don't know much about it myself. Maybe it's something we could look into together. We could start with that exhibit, down at the library."

The two of them turned to Sadie.

She smiled back at them. "Well, the opening is tonight," she said. "I'm sure you'd be much more than welcome. And you may want to take your time about telling the rest of your story. But as far as I'm concerned, what you just shared deserves just as a big a place in the Silver Peak local history as all the stories we've already got in the books about the famous Granby mill and construction company."

"Well, we'll have to see what we can do about that," Etta said, patting her daughter's hand. "Won't we?"

Beverly nodded.

"I just have to ask you one more question, Beverly," Sadie said.

"Anything," Beverly said. "I still feel so bad about how cold I've been."

"We're still trying to understand what happened to the instrument at the library," Sadie said. "Why anyone would want to do any damage to it. And it's clear how much you care about your mother, and how much you wanted to protect her from being upset by whatever the story behind the instrument was. I could understand it if you thought it might be better to see something happen to the instrument, than to have anything hurt your mother..."

Before Sadie could even finish her thought, Beverly began to shake her head. "No, no," she said. "I would never have done anything like that. I didn't want you to hurt Mom, and I didn't know the whole story of the instrument, and how it connected to our family history. But I loved it. And I knew Mom loved it. Doing anything to it would have hurt her too."

"Wait," Etta said. "Has something happened to the instrument?"

Quickly, Sadie explained the damage the instrument had suffered, and the fact that she believed she had been able to fully restore it.

"And you say that the damage occurred one evening this week?" Etta asked.

Sadie nodded.

"Then Beverly's got an airtight alibi," Etta said, and pointed at herself. "Me."

Sadie grinned at Etta's playful spirit. "And how is that?" she asked.

"They've been doing some work on my apartment at the home," Etta said. "So Beverly has very kindly been allowing me to have a weeklong sleepover here. We've been sharing her big old king-size bed, like a couple of schoolgirls. And I sleep even worse than the princess and the pea. There's no way she could have snuck out to damage that instrument without waking me up."

Sadie smiled. "I'm glad to hear it," she said. "And speaking of the library, I'd better get on my way. I'm supposed to help bake dozens and dozens of cookies for the event this evening. And I haven't even started yet."

"Well, you'd better get going," Etta said, waving her away. "We'll see you there!"

"Thank you," Sadie said, pausing to give each woman a warm handshake.

She walked back down Beverly's walk with a warm feeling for the first time that week. It had been amazing to hear the whole story of the instrument. And a week earlier, Kimama would have been overjoyed that Sadie had finally discovered it.

But now something else still nagged at Sadie too. Did anyone else know the story? And did it have anything to do with why anyone would ever want to damage the beautiful instrument? And, as the exhibit opening approached, whether they might try to harm it—or anything else—again?

23

"HOW MANY DOZEN COOKIES DID YOU PROMISE TO TAKE TO THE library?" Edwin asked. Despite the teasing protest in his voice, he was gamely helping, standing in Sadie's kitchen, carefully cutting leaf-shaped cookies out of the rolled dough, then setting them in precise lines on the cookie sheet she had set beside him while she worked on the next batch of dough.

She glanced over at him in amusement, both at his question, because she knew that his steel-trap mind had already filed the answer away the first time she told him, and by the incredible care with which he approached cookie baking.

"You do such an amazing job of cutting those out," Sadie said. "I think a materials management expert couldn't do better. You barely leave any scraps of dough at all."

"Waste not, want not," Edwin said.

"Well, don't make them too perfect," Sadie said. "I promised them homemade. They're going to think I cheated and just went to the store and bought a few bags."

"Not of these," Edwin said, shaking his head. "You couldn't get this recipe off a grocery store shelf."

"That's sweet," Sadie said, coming over to give him a kiss on the cheek.

As she did, Hank snuck in between them, hoping for a dropped scrap.

"Hank!" Sadie said, swatting him out of the way. "I swear, he begs more for cookie dough than he does for raw meat."

"Smart dog," Edwin said, popping a scrap of cookie dough into his own mouth, and smiling at the taste. "I don't care for raw meat much myself."

With Hank out of the way, Sadie delivered the kiss to Edwin's cheek, then went back to her post at the mixer, where she had been turning out batch after batch of dough.

As she did, she caught sight of Hank trotting out of the room, his tail held high and wagging, as he did when he'd discovered an especially pleasing treat.

"Edwin," Sadie said. "Please tell me you did not just feed the dog cookie dough."

Edwin was usually so dignified that the sheepish look on his face now filled her with delight. "I'm afraid I'll have to plead guilty to that," he said. "And beg for the judge's leniency."

"No leniency here," she said. "In fact, I'm assigning you to a work team. Your debt to society won't be paid off until you finish baking all of these cookies."

"Well," Edwin said, "that sounds about like time served to me. Since I already agreed to stay until we finish baking all these cookies."

"What can I say?" Sadie said. "I've always thought we'd get along better if we showed lawbreakers some mercy, and gave them a chance to give back to society."

"You're certainly going to be giving to society tonight," Edwin said. "I think there's going to be at least one cookie for everyone in Silver Peak."

"That won't be enough," Sadie said. "These are so delicious, they're all going to want two or three."

"It looks like it's going to be a long afternoon," said Edwin. "Good thing I'm in good company."

Sadie took a deep breath. "I'm glad you're here too," she said. "And to tell you the truth, I'm glad to be making all of these cookies. At least when you finish baking a cookie, you know it's done, and done right. But with this thing that happened over at the library with the instrument—no matter how much I learn, it just seems like I learn more I don't know."

"Well, have you considered motive?" Edwin asked. "It's key to any criminal trial. And I've watched a lot of investigators spend a lot of time on the evidence, without thinking enough about the human elements."

"That's a good thought," Sadie said. "So instead of trying to guess what happened, think about why it might have."

"Exactly," Edwin said.

"It's just so hard for me to think of why anybody would want to damage such a beautiful thing," Sadie said.

"Are you sure that's what happened?" Edwin asked.

"I guess not," Sadie said. "I mean, it could have been an accident, I guess." She glanced at Edwin for confirmation.

"Your guess is as good as mine," he said with an encouraging shrug. "Don't worry so much about whether the answer is right or not. Just treat it like a game. You're not trying to find out the truth. You're just thinking up a good story."

"Okay," Sadie said, "let me see. I guess…someone might want to hurt the instrument if they were angry at the Granby family."

Edwin nodded.

"But who in town would be angry at them?" Sadie asked.

"You don't have to figure that out right now," Edwin said. "You're just thinking up motives, not trying to solve the whole thing."

"All right," said Sadie. "Or if they were angry at the library. Or if they had something against natives, or native culture."

"Now you're thinking," Edwin said.

Sadie cracked two more eggs into the bowl as she reeled off ideas. "I'm going to think up motives for how it might have gotten damaged by accident. Even if they didn't mean to hurt it," she said.

Edwin nodded with a gesture that she suspected was very much like the one he used to use to give trial lawyers to continue their arguments.

"They might have been trying to steal it," she said. "Or even protect it."

"And why would they steal it?" Edwin asked.

"Because they wanted it," Sadie said. "Or…to embarrass the library. Or because they needed money. Speaking of which…"

"What?" Edwin said.

"I saw a strange thing downtown," Sadie said.

Edwin's eyebrows jumped. "Something that may have to do with the instrument and the library?" he said.

"I'm afraid so," Sadie said. "Although I hate to say it. It was Spike Harris's friend Steven. He's a gifted jeweler, and he works down at Bless Our Souls jewelry. And according to Spike, he's been having a hard time financially recently."

"What was he doing?" Edwin asked, his eyes narrowing as if she'd just stumbled on an important part of the argument.

"He was carrying a big package down the street," Sadie said. "It was so big that I went over to say hello to him. And when I did, I could see native markings on it."

"On what?" Edwin asked.

"I couldn't tell," Sadie said. "It was all wrapped in paper. But it was clearly a native artifact. So I followed him to his car…"

"Good, good," Edwin said.

Sadie was amused. She had been a little embarrassed to admit to following one of her fellow townspeople around the quiet streets of Silver Peak, but Edwin appeared to be treating this as if it was a routine part of standard police work—forgetting, for the moment, that she was not actually a policewoman.

"And when he got to his car, he put the package in the trunk. And I could see that his whole trunk was full of other native artifacts."

"Where did he take them?" Edwin asked.

"I don't know," Sadie said. "He drove off, and that was it."

Edwin clearly had something to say, and was just as clearly trying to resist saying it.

"What?" Sadie asked.

Edwin shook his head. "It might have been good to follow him," he said finally.

"I was on foot!" Sadie objected. "And he was already in his car."

"It all sounds very suspicious to me," Edwin said. "I think it's worth looking into."

"Believe me," Sadie said, "I'm planning on it. Just as soon as we finish these cookies." As she said this, she tapped the bottle of cinnamon in her hand, trying to urge out enough to complete the tablespoon in her hand.

Then she tapped again.

The box was empty.

"Are you out?" Edwin said.

"I'm never out of cinnamon," Sadie proclaimed, sailing with a victorious air to the cabinet where she stored extra baking supplies that she bought in quantity whenever she caught them on a good sale. But although she pushed aside the soft bags of flour, tins of baking powder, and tubs of icing, she couldn't find a single bottle of cinnamon.

She turned back to Edwin. "I'm out of cinnamon," she said.

He smiled.

"It's the most important ingredient in this recipe," she said. "That's probably how I ran through so much of it without noticing. I'm sorry, I'm going to have to go to the store to get some more."

"I'll hold down the fort," Edwin said.

"Thank you so much," she said, untying her apron and draping it over the back of a nearby chair.

"I'll take my hazard pay in cookies," Edwin said. "I'd say a few dozen should do."

"You better not!" Sadie warned, as she picked up her keys and slung her purse over her shoulder. "You're worse than Hank!"

"Be safe. I'll see you soon," Edwin called as she walked out the door.

A few minutes later, she was standing in the checkout lane at the Market, Silver Peak's only grocery store, holding four new tins of cinnamon, as well as several cans of creamed corn, which she'd picked up on impulse as she went by the aisle, since it had always been a favorite of hers.

At the register, she was glad to see Maggie, one of the owners of the Market, along with her husband, Lou.

"Sadie!" Maggie said. "It's so good to see you. I heard you're working on that big exhibit with the celebration tonight, over at the library."

"Well, right now, what I'm doing is baking cookies," Sadie said. "And I'm afraid I'm not the expert there that you are."

Maggie smiled. She had been a pastry chef in New York City, and the desserts that she made for the bakery at the Market were the stuff of legend in Silver Peak.

"What are you making?" she asked.

"One of my mother's old recipes," Sadie said. "Just a simple, delicious cookie. The problem is, we're trying to make twelve dozen of them."

"That explains all the cinnamon," Maggie said.

Sadie nodded. "I've never run out of it in the midst of baking before," she said.

"And you're determined not to do it again, I see," Maggie said, swiping the fourth tin of cinnamon over the price reader.

"Not if I can help it," Sadie said.

Maggie swiped a can of corn over the scanner. "I'm surprised you found some of this back there," she said. "Someone completely wiped us out of it earlier in the week."

Sadie's mind flashed back to the overflowing bins of canned donations at the library. "How many cans do you have to buy to buy out the whole store?" she asked.

"About a hundred," Maggie said. "At least at this store. But she didn't just get corn. She bought chili too."

A shiver went down Sadie's spine. "Do you remember who bought it?" she asked.

"Sure," Maggie said, with a grin. Then the grin faded for a minute, and she laughed ruefully. "I remember exactly who it is," she said. "I just don't remember her name."

Sadie paid for her groceries, to give Maggie a chance to think.

"But I'm sure you'd know her if you saw her," Maggie said. "She's a real nice gal, not too old, maybe in her thirties. Real pretty red hair. I always tell my redheads if they're lucky, they'll grow up to look like her. They've got to stick together, you know, reds."

Sadie laughed, but her mind was calculating quickly. "Is her hair short or long?" she asked.

"Good question," Maggie said. "It's short. Curly. A real nice cut, so I'm always noticing her earrings."

"Was it Genevieve Lakier?" Sadie asked.

Maggie's face lit up. "That's it!" she said. "I can't believe I forgot. I only check her driver's license twice a week."

"She's the one who bought all the corn, and the chili?" Sadie asked.

Maggie nodded vigorously. "Two hundred cans," she said. "I had to send out three bagboys with her, just to make sure she didn't strain her back getting it all in the car. Those cans are heavy."

"I bet," Sadie said.

"I was teasing her about how big a party she'd need to have to eat all that. Or how she wasn't going to need to come back here and shop until summer, if it was just her and her husband, eating all that. But it was that food drive," Maggie said. "She told me she was just going to take it all right over to the library. I do like to see that, though," she added. "It gives you a good feeling. And from our side, it's good for business!"

As the receipt finished printing, she tore it off and handed it to Sadie.

"Anything else I can do for you today?" Maggie asked.

Sadie shook her head as she collected her bag. "You've helped more than you know," she said.

"Well, I'll take that," Maggie said, turning to welcome the next customer.

Sadie walked out of the store, her mind abuzz. If Genevieve was the one who had left the cans, she would have been the person who was at the library closest to the time that the damage had been done to the instrument. *Maybe she had seen something that would help them understand what had happened,* Sadie thought.

Or maybe, she realized with a sudden start, Genevieve had actually had something to do with it.

In any case, she'd be able to talk with her soon. She knew she'd see her that night, at the exhibit opening.

24

"THERE'S NOTHING IN THIS WHOLE WIDE WORLD," SPIKE YODELED from the stage that had been set up in the library for the exhibit celebration, "like a Colorado girl."

It was one of the big hits of his band, the Skylarks, and they tore through it with a playful energy that promised good things for the show they were rehearsing to play in just an hour or so.

The doors hadn't been opened to the public yet, but already the library was far more crowded than usual, not just with the band, but with the volunteers Kimama had recruited to help with food and crowd flow and about a dozen local natives who had agreed to be on hand to talk with visitors about how the artifacts on display weren't just evidence of lost civilizations, but part of a rich culture that was still alive and vibrant in the present day.

"It looks pretty good, doesn't it?" James asked proudly. He was the one who had opened the door to Sadie's knock.

"It does," Sadie said, looking around the room with a feeling of satisfaction. The exhibit looked beautiful. Nothing had happened to any other artifacts since the strange occurrences at the library. And it was clearly getting set to be a great party.

She even caught sight of the display Genevieve Lakier had created from the quilts Sadie had lent her from her own shop. And even from a distance, Sadie could see that Genevieve had done a great job. The case Kimama had given her to fill was beautifully decorated, with each individual piece well supported and lit, and all the pieces arranged in a pleasing whole. Sadie could also see neatly typed cards identifying each quilt—the result, she was sure, of careful research on Genevieve's part. Sadie was eager to go over and get a look at it. It was possible she might even learn something about the items that had been in her shop from the research that Genevieve had done for this exhibit. Or that she might even learn something new about Silver Peak.

Still, she felt uneasy. Since they didn't know who had damaged the instrument, or moved around the boxes, they couldn't be sure why any of it had happened—or that it wouldn't again. And in the midst of a party, where hundreds of visitors would flow through the place, it would be very hard to keep a close eye on absolutely everything.

James was still beside her, staring out at all the activity.

"You've helped put together a beautiful event," she said. "I'm looking forward to it."

As she said it, she caught sight of Kimama in the crowd. She was talking with a tall man who had his back to her. But something about him seemed eerily familiar to Sadie. And when he turned his head, gesturing at something in the course of their conversation, Sadie knew why: it was Steven, Spike's friend.

And if her eyes didn't deceive her, he was holding a native artifact in his hands. When he should have no reason to be there, since, as Spike had said, he wasn't a member of the band.

Her unease growing, Sadie smiled at James. "Excuse me," she said. "I'm just going to have a word with Kimama."

"Sure," James said, nodding. "Hope you have a good time tonight."

"You too," Sadie said and headed into the crowd toward the exhibit, where Kimama was standing with Steven.

When she finally reached them, Kimama greeted her with a big smile. "Sadie, it's great to see you! Have you met Steven?"

Sadie's heart sank at the thought of having to deflate Kimama's obviously delighted mood. But at this point, nothing was worth taking a risk with the exhibit. And from what she had seen and heard, Steven definitely posed a risk to the exhibit.

Sadie glanced down at the object in Steven's hands, a large, beautifully painted earthen jar.

"We have met," Sadie said, trying to keep her tone friendly, despite her suspicions. "Over at Bless Our Souls. And earlier today."

"That's right," Steven said.

Sadie tried to read his face, looking for any hint of the evasiveness she had seen earlier in the day. But she didn't see any. He just seemed like the friendly, open guy she'd met earlier, at Bless Our Souls, with the affection for native culture, and a knack for making jewelry.

"What are you doing here?" she asked, and looked pointedly at the object in his hands. "And what is that doing out of the exhibit?"

"Isn't it a wonderful piece?" Kimama asked. "We are so lucky to have it."

Sadie continued to watch Steven like a hawk. "I'm sure we are," she said. "I'm afraid I just don't understand why it's not in the cases, with the others."

Kimama gave Steven a smile. "Sadie's always looking out for the objects," she said. "She's been helping us make sure that we're able to take the very best care of everything. As you can see."

She turned her smile on Sadie. "It's not in the case because we haven't found a place for it yet," she said.

"Oh?" Sadie asked.

"It's a new collection," Kimama told Sadie, her eyes shining. "From my own family. These are things that have been in my family for years. They're part of my own history, and also the history of all my people. And of Silver Peak. But, of course, it's very precious to my family. And they don't just belong to me. I had to negotiate with my own relatives, and also with some of the leaders of my people.

"I wasn't sure if I could get it until the last minute. And I didn't want to embarrass my family, or the library, by announcing it if it wasn't going to be able to happen. That's why I hadn't mentioned it to anyone yet. But Steven knows my uncle, who is the one who put all this together. He's one of the area experts on native culture. And he's been the one in our generation who served as the caretaker of all these things. He's restored some of them, and identified others. And he keeps them safe and well-preserved, and introduces them to the children in our families, so they can get a sense of who they are, and where they come from. Since Steven already had a connection with him, Steven has been helping me get everything together, as quietly as possible."

Sadie's eyes widened in understanding. "So that's why you didn't want to talk much about that big package you were carrying on the street," she said to Steven.

"I'm sorry about that," he said. "Usually I would have loved to have stopped to talk with you about it. In fact, I'd probably have gone on and on until you were bored. But I couldn't this time. Kimama swore me to secrecy."

Kimama stepped back to reveal a whole new case that had just been installed since the last time Sadie was there. The new collection almost doubled the number of objects that had originally been on display. And Sadie could see at a glance that they were of enormously high quality. And that the selection was highly varied—everything from rough-hewn bowls, to drawings, to well-worn drums, to regalia made from impressive feathers, beads, and fringes. She was even delighted to see what looked like intricately beaded ceremonial garb created for a child who, by the size, couldn't be older than two or three.

"I'm so pleased with it," Kimama said, gesturing toward the bounty of beautiful objects. "It means so much to me to have things from my own family as part of the exhibit. And not just from my family, but from our people. Things that are still part of our legacy today. So many of the items I've been able to display here are things that had wound up in the hands of the families of settlers."

"Like the Granby family instrument," Sadie said.

"Exactly," Kimama said. "So these things are special to me for many reasons. They're part of a living history, objects that have been passed down through my family for generations."

She looked down into the case. "And this case is going to be permanent," she said, "even when this exhibit is over. The library board has talked about it, and they feel this exhibit has been an important part of the identity of the library, and the town. And that the history isn't just for Thanksgiving. It's a foundational part of the story of Colorado. So this display will hold items that represent the culture of local native people year-round, from now on."

"That's wonderful," Sadie said. "We're very fortunate to have you in Silver Peak, Kimama."

Kimama beamed, and the two women embraced.

Then Sadie looked across the crowd to where Spike was warming up. The whole band had dropped out, and now he was checking the sound of the instrument that had caused them so much consternation and trouble that week. It still sounded beautiful, even with the repairs.

"You'd barely know anything had happened to it," Kimama said.

"I'm so glad," Sadie said. "But I still wish we knew what had."

"Me too," Kimama said. "And we also never solved the mystery of the overflowing donation boxes. But I guess that's a problem I shouldn't worry about solving. It's a good one to have."

As she spoke, one of the staff members unlocked the library doors, and the crowd that had gathered outside began to swarm in: young families with kids, customers Sadie recognized from her store, and friends she knew from church—or from even further back, to the days when she had lived in Silver Peak as a girl.

"And we'll have to wait until the party's over to work on that," Kimama said with a rueful glance.

Then, among the gathering crowd, Sadie picked out one more face. Genevieve Lakier had just entered, her unmistakable curly red hair a standout, even in the big crowd. She was glancing around with an expression that showed both eagerness and satisfaction. The satisfaction of a job well done, Sadie guessed. And eagerness to see it, and have others see it, in all its glory.

Sadie glanced from Genevieve, back to Kimama, and smiled.

"Maybe not," she said.

25

"I COULDN'T HAVE DONE IT BETTER MYSELF," SADIE SAID, WHEN she caught up with Genevieve in front of the case full of quilts.

Genevieve turned around. When she saw Sadie, her face broke into a wide smile. Instead of saying anything, she just enveloped Sadie in a big hug.

Sadie patted her on the back, then released her.

"Isn't it wonderful?" Genevieve said. "I couldn't be more pleased with it."

"It looks even better up close," Sadie said, surveying the contents of the case. It wasn't easy to get the feel of a quilt without hanging the whole thing up on a wall, which obviously there wasn't room for in the library, along with everything else that was on display that evening. But Genevieve had done a masterly job arranging the quilts to show off their most interesting elements, as well as give a substantial glimpse of their overall pattern. "You've done a wonderful job of showing these off to their best advantage. I think maybe your skills were wasted in event planning. Perhaps we ought to be thinking about trying to find you something in design."

"Don't be fooled," Genevieve said. "Event planning is all about design. That's where I learned these skills. It's just that in event planning, all of your elements are moving. You can put a daub of paint on a page, and expect it to stay still. But put a person in a room and…" She shrugged in mock defeat.

Sadie laughed.

"So making an arrangement of things that aren't going to get up and walk away after you put them in their place"—Genevieve spread her hands—"is child's play."

"Well, you say that," Sadie said. "But not everybody could have made the case look as good as this."

"Thanks for saying that," Genevieve said. "I appreciate it. And I did enjoy getting the chance to put my rusty skills to work again. But don't forget, I couldn't have done it if I didn't already have such good raw materials to work with. This exhibit depends on the quality of the quilts. I couldn't make them look this good if they weren't so well-chosen to begin with. And I've got you to thank for that."

"I'm just glad to see them get out of the back of the store for a change," Sadie said. "And this is a wonderful advertisement for the Antique Mine."

"I hope so," Genevieve said. "You know you've got me hooked as a customer, at least."

"And I'm very happy to have you," Sadie said. She looked back at the display, and her eye fell on one of the cards, explaining how native women had adapted the traditional American Lone Star pattern into a Morning Star pattern that reflected their own beliefs and traditions. "I think it's very touching that you chose these quilts as the point of connection between settlers and native people. So much of the history that we hear is of men, and so much of it is about trade or fighting, when people are at odds with each other, or even doing each other harm. But this shows the history of the women of both people. And how they were learning from each other, and sharing, at the same time. I think it's a very important part of the history."

"I'm glad you think so," Genevieve said. "I think I might have had some ideas about that myself, at some point in the game. But by now, I'm just glad the exhibit is finally opening. I think I may have spent more time at the library in the past few days than I did at home, getting this all set up."

Sadie saw her opportunity, and jumped at it. "And you were here earlier in the week also," she said, with a smile that she hoped would invite Genevieve's confidence. "I hear you were responsible for a record-breaking donation to the food drive."

Genevieve gave her a funny look. She looked uncomfortable. Quickly, Sadie's mind began to calculate. After all, Genevieve had had access to the library for a good part of the week, in order to put her part of the exhibit together. Was it possible that she had something to do with the damage to the instrument? Or the mischief that happened later, in the library storage room?

"It seems like such a lot of food," Sadie said. "Why would you bring it in the middle of the night?"

Genevieve's eyes darted around the crowd, as if looking for help. But then they met Sadie's again. She took a deep breath. "We went through a hard time last year," she said. "My husband and I. I'd never had to go on any kind of public assistance before. I never thought I'd have to. But we were in bad trouble. We needed to do anything we could to take care of our kids. So for a good part of the winter, we got a lot of our food from the food pantry. And I swore then that when I was in a position to pay them back, I would. Things have been better this year. Not better enough that I can make a big donation to them. But enough that I had a little extra I could spend when I saw the food drive signs go up. And the creamed corn and chili were the things my kids liked best, when we'd be getting food from the pantry. So I just went over to the Market, and loaded up on all of it I could find.

"But I didn't want anyone to know," she said. "I guess it's foolish, but it's still hard for me to talk about how bad it got for us last year. And I think it's better, if you're going to try to do something for somebody, not to let the whole world know. It's between me and God, not me and other people. At least that's the way I think about it. So I thought, let me just see if it's open at night. And it was. So I was able to deliver everything without anyone else having to know about it."

She paused, then cocked her head to look at Sadie. "Why do you ask?"

"It's just been a little mystery around here," Sadie said. "The donation buckets have been filling up much more quickly than usual. And that front door isn't supposed to be unlocked after business hours."

"It's not?" Genevieve said. "But I thought it was so convenient. Especially for families that work. I actually told several friends about it, how thoughtful it was of them to think of that. A couple of my friends were going to come by the next day with after-hours drop-offs."

Sadie nodded. "That explains a lot," she said.

"Explains what?" Genevieve asked.

"The library had an unexpectedly large batch of donations the day after yours arrived, as well," Sadie said. "Probably from your friends."

"I guess so," Genevieve said. "I hope I haven't caused any problems. I was only trying to help people get their food in for the drive."

"Oh," Sadie said, "I don't think the people running the drive think of too much food as a problem. I wouldn't worry too much about it."

Genevieve smiled, relieved.

"There is one thing, though," Sadie said.

"What's that?" Genevieve asked.

"While you were here dropping off your food," Sadie said. "You must have been here for a little while. You would have had to make several trips, to fill up all the bins."

"I did," Genevieve said.

"Did you notice anything?" Sadie asked.

"Like what?" Genevieve asked.

"About the library," Sadie said. "Anything different? Out of place?"

Genevieve frowned. "I don't know…," she said. Then her expression brightened. "I do remember one thing. I don't know that it was out of place, exactly. I actually thought it was kind of sweet."

"What was that?" Sadie asked.

"There was someone in the library, still," Genevieve said. "Working."

Sadie's heart skipped a beat. This was the first time anyone had actually gotten a look at whoever might have done the damage to the instrument. "What time did you say you arrived?" Sadie asked.

"Let's see…," Genevieve said. "I had managed to get the kids to bed. So it would have been after ten. And then I had to get everything into the car and bring it over here. I'd say it was sometime just before eleven."

Sadie nodded. "And do you remember anything about the person you saw?"

"It was still pretty dark," Genevieve said. "I guess he didn't want to give anyone the mistaken impression that the library was still open, so the overhead lights weren't on, of course. But he seemed to be working pretty hard."

"What did he look like?" Sadie asked.

"He had dark hair," Genevieve said. "Straight."

"Was he young?" Sadie said. "Old? Did you see the color of his eyes?"

Genevieve shook her head. "I couldn't see much at all," she said. "He seemed to be doing something in the back of the library. My guess was that it had something to do with the exhibit. So it was too far away for me to see much."

Or for whoever it was to see that he was being observed, Sadie thought.

Then Genevieve's eyes grew wide. "Oh!" she said. "I do remember one thing."

"What's that?" Sadie asked.

"He was wearing a jacket," Genevieve said. "Dark, like a jeans jacket. But with a shearling collar."

Sadie's mind flashed back to the jacket she'd seen James wearing the morning of the big can delivery. She glanced around the library, trying to catch a glimpse of him, but he was nowhere to be found.

26

SADIE PUSHED THROUGH THE ENTHUSIASTIC CROWD, LEAVING Genevieve, whom she'd just excused herself from, behind. All around her, people were *ooh*ing and *ahh*ing over the beautiful objects and the scope of the exhibit.

"I never knew that," she heard one man say to his wife.

"Well, keep looking, honey," said his wife. "I'm sure it's not the only thing we can learn here tonight."

But when Sadie got to the spot where she'd last seen James, just inside the door, she still hadn't caught sight of him anywhere in the library.

When she reached the door, she went out, through the little lobby, and onto the front steps. The huge wave of people who had flowed in as the exhibit opened had slowed to a trickle, so she was able to spend a little time fiddling with the lock. Quickly, she discovered that if she locked the door from within, then pushed the door, it still swung open. The handle swung around on the lock, making it look for all the world as if it was securely fastened. But it wasn't.

That meant that if someone had tried to lock the outer door of the library from within, the door would still be open to the public.

Senses tingling, Sadie checked the inner door. That one worked just as it ought to. So it was only the outer door that was insecure, Sadie reasoned. And it must lock securely when locked from the outside, as Kimama had said she did each day when she left. She knew Kimama well enough to know that she would never leave her beloved library open day after day without a quick tug on the door to make sure it was closed after she locked it.

In fact, it was a problem with the lock that might have gone for some time without anyone noticing, because Kimama always locked the building from the outside. It was only a problem that would emerge if someone who had keys to the library tried to lock themselves in after hours.

And it was a problem that might never have been discovered if the food drive hadn't been running at the same time that person locked themselves in. Because otherwise, especially with the book return available from outside, few people would have had any reason to try to get into the library lobby at all.

Sadie slipped back into the library. As she did, she ran into Kimama near the front counter.

"I've just learned a few things," Sadie said. "About the night the instrument was damaged."

"What did you find out?" Kimama asked, drawing her over into a corner.

Quickly, Sadie described what she'd discovered about Genevieve's delivery of the groceries, and the broken front door lock.

"I'll get someone out to fix that right away," Kimama said. "But you say the inside door was still effectively locked?"

"As far as I can tell," Sadie said. "No one without keys could have gotten in. But…"

"What?" Kimama asked.

"Someone with keys still might have."

"Well, of course," Kimama said, her expression confused. "Anyone with keys could get into the library at any time. But I'm the only one who has a set of keys."

"Are you sure about that?" Sadie asked.

"Why do you ask?" Kimama said.

Sadie sighed. "Because Genevieve saw someone inside the night she brought her food donation in."

"Did she get a good look?" Kimama asked. "Could she see who it was?"

"She told me it was dark, so she wasn't certain," Sadie said. "But she thought he was wearing a jeans jacket. With a shearling collar."

"James," Kimama breathed. Suddenly, she was scanning the library with the same intensity that Sadie had been just a few minutes before. But despite the fact that there were now two of them, neither of them could catch sight of him.

"There must be some kind of explanation," Kimama said. "Or maybe she saw something that looked like a shearling jacket…"

"Did James have access to your keys?" Sadie asked.

Kimama shook her head. "I take them home with me every night. They go out the door with me, as you know. Because I always lock the place up on my way out."

"Are there any other sets of keys?" Sadie asked.

Kimama began to shake her head. Then her eyes widened. "Yes," she said. "I have two spare sets. I keep one at home. And there's one in my desk, in case anything happens."

"Did James know about them?" Sadie asked.

Kimama took a deep breath. "I can't say for sure," she said. "But I did have him doing projects relatively frequently at my desk. And they wouldn't have been hard to discover. They're just in the main drawer, beside the pens."

Sadie loved the fact that people in Silver Peak didn't worry much about crime, the way people did in big cities. But sometimes that lack of concern left them open to problems of their own.

"It sounds like maybe he helped himself to them that night," she said. "And perhaps the night after, when the storage room was rifled through."

"But why?" Kimama asked. "James loves these things. If anything, he's more passionate about our history than me."

"I don't know," said Sadie. "We'll have to ask him."

"Well, to do that, we have to find him," Kimama said grimly.

But as she took her first determined step into the crowd, Spike came rushing up, Steven close behind him.

"You have the instrument," Spike said breathlessly. "You have it, right? I'm sorry, I only left it alone for a minute. But I can see why you'd pick it up. It only makes sense not to let it out of our sight, after everything that's happened. It's just that we're about to play. So I need it back."

Sadie felt a sinking feeling in her stomach. She didn't have to have spent every minute with Kimama to know that Kimama hadn't picked up the instrument. Someone else had. She could see it from the expression of horror that began to spread over Kimama's face.

27

"Not again...," Kimama groaned.

"What?" Spike said, confused.

"Kimama doesn't have the instrument," Sadie explained to Spike.

"Well, then, where is...," Spike began.

Kimama broke in, taking control of the unwinding situation. "Where did you leave it?" she asked.

Spike pointed back to the storage room. "In the storage room," he said. "I hadn't wanted to let it out of my sight, but I didn't want to leave it up on stage either. We try to keep people away from our instruments, but you can never tell what's going to happen before a show. Especially with this many little kids in the audience. I just didn't want to take any chances with it."

Kimama had already started to stride toward the storage room, a small parade trailing behind her, composed of Sadie, Spike, and Steven.

"We had worked it all out," Steven said. "I was going to go back and get it from the storage room at the last minute before he had to play. He told me exactly what songs led up to the one he needed the instrument for, so I could follow along in the set. So there would be the least chance of anyone getting their hands on it. Or of it getting damaged."

By this time, they had reached the storage room. Kimama took a few steps around it, then whirled back. "Where did you leave it?" she asked.

"Just right here," Spike said. "On the main table."

He pointed to an empty space, surrounded by neatly arranged stacks of papers and materials for the exhibit.

Beside him, Steven nodded. "That's exactly right," he said. "I was with him when he did it."

"Did you search the room?" Kimama asked.

Spike shook his head. "I didn't think it was gone," he said. "My first thought was that you must have it."

"Well, that would have been nice," Kimama said. "But that's not what happened."

Together, the four of them searched quickly through the stacks of boxes, opening up anything that might have been big enough to hide the instrument. Sadie's heart was in her throat the whole time, afraid that this time they'd find it again in actual splinters.

"Nothing," Kimama said finally, when every box had been unstacked or overturned.

"That's almost a relief," Sadie said. "At least we didn't find it in pieces."

"Yet," Kimama muttered.

As she did, the storage room door opened, and James came in. He had a quizzical look on his face. "There you are," he said. "Sorry, was there a meeting I missed?"

"Where have you been?" Kimama asked.

"They sent me to look for you," James said. "Genevieve is ready to get things started, but they needed you to open everything up, and they couldn't find the leader of the band."

"I was looking for you earlier," Kimama said. "Sadie and I both were. Neither of us could find you."

"Oh," James said. "Yeah, I went out. Genevieve needed me to get some more refreshments. I guess whoever promised to bring the drinks forgot they also were supposed to buy ice."

"James," Sadie said. "The instrument has gone missing."

James dropped his eyes to the ground. "Wow," he said. "That's terrible."

"There's something else," Sadie said. "We found out who left the cans here the night that the instrument was damaged. It was Genevieve Lakier."

James looked up at her again, but now he was visibly nervous. "That's great," he said. "I mean, isn't it? She gave a lot of food."

"She did," Sadie said, nodding. "But she also came late at night. Around eleven. And she said she saw somebody still working here at the library."

"Nobody's authorized to be in the library that late," Kimama said. "And I certainly wasn't there to supervise anyone."

"Huh," James said, studying his shoes again.

"James," Sadie said. "Genevieve said the person she saw was wearing a jacket very much like yours."

"That's weird," James said.

"It's very strange," Kimama said. "And I'm afraid that, since you and the instrument disappeared from the library today around the same time, I'm going to have to ask you a few questions."

"Okay," James said tentatively.

"To start with," Kimama said. "I'd like to take a look at your car. Just to make sure that the instrument didn't get misplaced somehow."

James took a deep breath. He lifted his hand to his face. Then he let it drop.

"I never meant for it to get hurt," he said.

"Has something happened to it?" Kimama demanded.

"No," James said. "Not this time. It's out in my car. It's fine."

"Except that it's out in your car," Kimama said. "And not here in the library for the exhibit. Where it belongs." She crossed her arms, the disappointment on her face unmistakable.

James didn't seem to be able to bear looking at it. He dropped his gaze to his feet again.

"James," Kimama said, "I don't understand. You've been such a great help here. And I know you care about this history. What in the world would possess you to do such a thing?"

James took a deep breath. Then he sank down on a nearby box, his head in his hands.

After a long minute, he finally looked up. "I'm sorry," he said. "I'll tell you everything."

28

But after he said this, James didn't seem to know where to start. Everyone in the room was silent and frozen, staring at him.

Finally, he said, "That instrument belongs in my family. The man who made it was Ute."

"The song written on it," Sadie said, quickly putting together the face of James's heritage and the fact that Dr. Gramas's friend had recognized the decorative writing on the front as actually being some kind of musical notation. "Did you recognize it?"

James shook his head. "I can't read Ute," he said. "Not many of us can. But I know the story."

"What story is that?" Kimama asked.

"Of the instrument," James said.

Sadie thought back to Professor Kilgore, and how he'd told her that the story of the abduction of Agatha Barnhill had come down through the local native community as well, but in a very different form than the one in which it had appeared in the papers at the time. "It came down as part of your history?" Sadie asked.

For the first time, James looked up. "Of my family history," he said.

"Your family history," Kimama repeated. "What do you mean?"

"My ancestor made that instrument," James said. "He was a Ute chief. One of the last ones to lead us before we were forced on to reservation lands. He died when soldiers attacked his peaceful camp. They took his bride and one of his sons captive. And they stole the instrument."

"He had more than one son?" Sadie asked. "I thought only one survived."

"Wait," Kimama said. "Who are we talking about?"

"The man who made the instrument," Sadie told her. "He made it for his wife, who was a daughter of the Granby family."

"So that's how the instrument got into their hands," Kimama said.

Sadie nodded. "But Candace and Beverly never knew that history," she said. "Until we started looking into it. I just heard it myself for the first time today. The chief's son was Beverly's grandfather."

James stood up. "The other son was my great-great-grandfather," he said.

"So he survived," Sadie breathed. "Without his mother... or his father?"

James nodded. "His aunt was just a girl herself," he said. "But she saw him running away from the battle, and she caught up with him and protected him. They almost got killed by a pair of soldiers, but at the last minute another one rode up and told them they couldn't harm the children. They wanted to get past him, but he stood in front of them, on his horse, until she was able to slip away into the woods."

"How old was your great-grandfather at that time?" Sadie asked.

"Only about six or seven," James said. "And a little while later, he moved, with the rest of our people who remained, to the reservation. But he never forgot his father, or his mother. And he always talked about the instrument."

"So you have musicians in your family from way back," Spike observed.

Even though he was obviously still very upset, James nodded with pride as he gave his answer. "Yes."

"I could tell it was in your blood, man," Spike said.

"I hear lots of stories about our people from the time before the settlers arrived," James said. "But this is the only one that I knew that was just about our family. And I knew the instrument was unusual. Because something of that kind is not usually part of our tradition. Although today I play the guitar. My grandfather taught me. So when Kimama began to talk about it, I was excited. And when I saw it, I knew it had to be ours."

"How did you know?" Kimama asked.

"From the initials inside," James said. "My great-great-grandfather never forgot his mother's name. So it's been passed down through our family."

"But, James," Kimama said, the hurt in her voice evident, "why did you do what you did? I know what it's like to feel that something belongs to your people, and not the people who have it. Sometimes it's even hard for me to do the work I need to do, to put this exhibit together. Because I can't help but think of all the history that brought us here. But no matter how it may seem, these things don't just belong to us and our family. They belong to all of our people, all natives. And with this instrument, it sounds like it does belong in part to the Granby family. Their kin and their blood have a claim on it too. Even if you felt it rightfully belonged to you, why would you do anything to harm it? Why would you try to destroy something of your own?"

"I didn't mean to!" James said. He had been holding himself together well until now, but suddenly his voice rose, and Sadie could hear the youth and boyishness in it.

"Then why did you?" Kimama asked.

James took a deep breath. "My grandfather," he said.

"Did he put you up to this?" Kimama said. "Did he ask you to do something to the instrument?"

James shook his head. "He doesn't even know about it," he said.

"Then what does he have to do with this?" Kimama asked.

"He's dying," James said. As he did, his voice cracked, and his eyes suddenly turned bright with tears. He blinked quickly to chase them away.

Kimama put her hand on his shoulder. "Oh, James," she said, "I'm so sorry."

"It's okay," James said, as he brought himself under control. "But nobody in our family loved the story as much as he did. He used to tell it and tell it. It was almost like it became one of the myths of our people to him. As if it might have some kind of special powers or magic to it.

"He's been so sick for so long," James said. "I didn't think the instrument was magic. But I've wanted to be able to do something for him for so long. And there was never anything I could do. So when the instrument came into the library, I thought, maybe I could just get it, and take it to him. I wasn't even going to give it to him. I just wanted him to have the chance to hold it, before he went."

"How did you get into the library after hours?" Kimama asked him.

"I took the keys from your desk," James said. "I'm sorry! I like working here. I like working for you. I like learning all the things I got to learn, about our history, and about all the other stories in all these books. But I thought I might even be able to get it over to him real early in the morning, and then bring it back before anyone noticed. I didn't think anyone would ever have to know."

"But you broke it," Kimama said, her voice full of reproach.

"I know!" James said. "I never meant to. I was trying to keep the lights low so that nobody would see I was in there from outside. But I guess it was too dark for me to realize that the case wasn't fastened all the way."

"I didn't fasten it," Spike said. "Because the storage space was on the ground. I'd just flip it open every day, and lift it out."

"I guess that's why," James said. "But like I said, I didn't notice until I'd picked the case up. And then I heard this terrible noise. And when I finally turned the lights on, there it was. In pieces."

The anguish in his eyes gave a strong indication of how he must have felt when he first saw the destruction.

Kimama shook her head. "Oh, James. And instead of telling us..."

"I didn't know what to do," James said. "I probably should have told you. But I was just so scared. And so I just picked it up as well as I could, and I hid it in another part of the room. I figured maybe if it was misplaced nobody would find it, and figure out what had happened."

"But we found it right away," said Sadie.

James nodded. "I'm so glad it was you, Mrs. Speers," he said. "And I'm so glad you were able to fix it. I would have given anything for that."

"I'm glad too," Sadie said.

"But what about the boxes that were moved around back here in the storage room," Kimama asked. "Did you have anything to do with that?"

James nodded. "Yes," he said. "That was me."

"But why?" Kimama said.

"I got scared," James said. "When you started trying to find out what happened, I thought if you figured out the history of the instrument, it would be too easy to connect it with me. So I wanted to make it seem as if someone was interested in the whole exhibit. I thought that would make it a lot harder to figure out who did it."

"That's true," Sadie said, with a sigh. "It did."

James turned to Spike. "I'm sorry, Spike. I know you felt awful about it getting damaged too."

Spike nodded.

"And where is the instrument now?" Kimama asked.

James's shoulders slumped. "It's out in my car," he said.

"After everything that happened," Kimama said, "you were still going to try to take it again?"

"I just really wanted my grandfather to have the chance to see it," James said. "To see it, and to hold it. I was going to sneak it back tonight. I thought, with so many people here, and with all the confusion, no one would guess that I took it. And nobody would be able to be sure that it hadn't just gotten misplaced in the confusion of the exhibit."

Kimama stood with her arms folded, staring at him.

"I'm sorry," he said. "I guess you have to fire me now. But I understand."

Kimama took a deep breath.

"Nobody said anything about firing you," she said. "How else am I going to make you work off all the trouble you're put us through?"

James raised his head, his eyes full of surprise. "Do you mean it?" he asked.

"And how am I supposed to put on this whole exhibit if I'm short-staffed?" Kimama continued.

James looked as if he couldn't believe his good fortune. "Uh…okay," he said, looking around as if he was trying to figure out what to do next.

"But I don't ever want to hear about your doing anything like this ever again," Kimama said. "And if I do, there will be consequences."

"I understand," James said. "I shouldn't ever have taken something that wasn't mine."

"Well," Kimama said, "this whole exhibit is about that question, isn't it? You and I both know that the question of who owns these things we're dealing with isn't simple. And it does sound like your family has a claim on that instrument. And a connection with one of the families in town that is probably worth exploring. We can talk about that later. What I'm talking about is the lying and the sneaking around. You should have come to me. You should have trusted me with what you were hoping to do. We could almost certainly have made something work."

James nodded.

As he did, the storage room door popped open, and Genevieve poked her head in. She looked at Spike with a twinkle in her eyes. "I declare," she said. "I'm always having to track down musicians in the strangest places to get an event started. But I didn't expect to find my client hiding out in the back room, as well," she added, with a glance at Kimama.

"Okay," Kimama said, clapping her hands together to signal it was time for action. "We've got the whole town of Silver Peak waiting for us out there. Time to go."

She caught the door to let Spike and Steven file out, then nodded for James to go out, as well. He darted for the door with one last bashful look at her. As Sadie began to follow him through it, Kimama put her hand on her shoulder.

"Thank you," she said.

"Thank you," Sadie said. "It's been an honor to work on this exhibit."

Genevieve gave a good-natured but increasingly impatient gesture toward the stage.

"I'll be right there," Kimama said, and followed her.

As Kimama took the stage to a huge roar of applause and began to welcome the crowd and talk about the history and highlights of the exhibit, Sadie made her way through the crowd, looking for Edwin.

It didn't take her long to find him, because his tall form towered over most of the other people in the crowd. She went up to him where he was standing at the refreshment table. As she came up, he popped a bite of cookie into his mouth, and then snapped to attention, like a young cadet in the presence of a general.

"Everything's in order here, ma'am," he said, as if giving a report to his superior officer. "A dozen spice cookies delivered, just like you asked."

Sadie gave him a wry smile and a peck on the cheek. "Thank you very much," she said. Then she glanced at the cookie in his hand. "But it appears that you've let someone make off with one of them."

"Oh no," Edwin said. "This here?"

He raised the cookie.

Sadie nodded.

Edwin shook his head. "You misunderstand," he said, looking at the cookie. "This is not an example of my careless guarding of the cookie. What you see here, instead, is quality control in action."

"You didn't think my cookies were going to be good enough?" Sadie teased. "You had to check?"

"You can't ever be too careful," Edwin said. "In fact, I think maybe I'd better try another. One for you?"

Sadie nodded happily, as the band took the stage.

29

THE OLD MAN SAT ON THE COUCH, WRAPPED IN A WARM BLANKET.

He was clearly ill, too ill to stand up.

But his eyes were full of life. And when the caught sight of his grandson, they were full of joy.

"Hi, Grandpa," James said, going over to greet the old man. When the two of them had clasped hands, James straightened up and turned back to the friends who had trailed in with him.

"I would like you to meet some people."

"Who are your friends?" the old man asked.

"This is Kimama," James said. "I work for her at the library. She just put together a big exhibit about the history of native people in this part of Colorado. Kimama, this is my grandfather, Benjamin Ouray."

"Welcome," Benjamin said, with a smile.

"This is Sadie," James said. "She helped us..." He paused for a moment, clearly trying to figure out how to sum up Sadie's role in the events of the past week. "With the exhibit," he finished.

"Wonderful," Benjamin said.

As Sadie and Kimama moved aside, Candace, Beverly, and Etta stepped forward, Etta in front, with a wide smile.

"Another young person," Benjamin said with a grin. "Just like me."

Etta clasped his hand, but as she did, she seemed to be overcome with emotion. Her eyes filled with tears.

Benjamin looked at James, his eyes questioning.

"This is Etta," James said. "And her daughter, Beverly. And *her* daughter, Candace."

Benjamin took them all in with a glance.

"Etta has something she'd like to tell you," James said.

"Please," Benjamin said, gesturing for Etta to take a seat beside him on the couch.

Etta sank down beside him, and took a deep breath. "It's very nice to meet you," she said, patting his hand. "I never thought..." She trailed off, unable to continue.

Again, Benjamin glanced at James.

As he did, Etta collected herself. "You see," she said, as Benjamin glanced back at her, "I believe that I'm a granddaughter of the Ouray family. My grandmother was Agatha Barnhill, who was married to one of your ancestors."

Benjamin's eyes widened. "The one who was taken by the soldiers?" he asked.

Etta nodded. "That's right," she said. "With her son. My father."

Tears now appeared in Benjamin's eyes. "We didn't know," he said. "We never knew if he lived or not. If she was able to protect him."

Etta nodded again, vigorously. "Yes, she did," she said. "She did everything she could to protect him. And then her family did the best they could to take care of him. My family," she added.

Benjamin took a deep breath. "Her brother was my grandfather," he said. "His relatives also protected him."

"I'm so glad to hear it," Etta said. "I'm so glad they did."

For a long moment, the two of them were silent, looking at each other.

"And that makes us relatives," Benjamin finally said.

"That's right," Etta said with delight. As she did, Beverly came over to her. She reached down to put one hand on Etta's shoulder, and linked the other around Candace's waist as Candace stood next to her.

"I'm afraid we don't know much," Etta said, "about the Ute people. But we'd like to learn. About them. And about you."

Benjamin shook his head gently. "Ute is the name they gave us," he said. "It's not what we call ourselves."

"Oh?" Candace asked. "What do you call yourselves? Ourselves," she corrected herself.

"*Nuche*," Benjamin said.

"Nuche?" Beverly repeated.

Benjamin nodded.

"What does it mean?" Etta asked.

"People of soul," he said. "People of substance."

"That's beautiful," Candace said.

Behind them, Kimama made a sound as she shuffled around with something.

"Grandpa," James said. "We have something we'd like to show to you."

"Oh?" Benjamin said with polite interest.

Kimama turned around, holding the instrument, which she handed to Etta.

"This has been in our family for a long time," she said.

"Do you remember the instrument, Grandpa?" James said. "The one that the chief made for Agatha?"

But it was clear from his grandfather's expression that something deep in the old man had already recognized the instrument, even before the explanation had been given to him. He gazed at it with disbelief, and wonder, and longing. But he didn't so much as raise a hand to touch it.

"It's meant a lot to our family," Etta said. "But I hear that it's also meant a great deal to yours."

"I've had dreams about this instrument," Benjamin said. "Ever since I was a young man. I've held all kinds of instruments in my hands. I've always hoped one of them might feel like this one, in my dreams. But nothing ever has."

"Well," Etta said, "we think we've had it long enough. We know that you're a musician, and so is your grandson, James. And we'd like you to have it."

Benjamin's eyes lit up as Etta held out the instrument, her hands quaking faintly.

When he held it for the first time in his hands, a wide grin spread across his face.

His hands were weathered and worn, and gnarled with arthritis so that Sadie wondered at first whether he'd even be able to move them to pluck at the strings.

But he curved first one finger, then the next, tamping down the strings against the neck.

Then he struck his first note.

When he heard it, he went perfectly still, listening until it vanished from the air completely.

Then he struck the note again.

After a few quick experiments, he managed to pick out a simple melody on the old instrument, which was so full of his story, and Silver Peak's.

Then he opened his mouth and began to sing.

About the Author

CAROLE JEFFERSON IS THE PEN NAME FOR A TEAM OF WRITERS who have come together to create the series Mysteries of Silver Peak. *Instrument of Peace* was written by Vera Dodge. Vera grew up in small towns in the Midwest. She lives and works in Brooklyn.

Flurries of Suspicion

"SADIE? ARE YOU HERE?"

Sadie smiled at the sound of Roz's voice and placed the lid back on the bottle of boiled linseed oil. "I'm in the back room," she called out. "Be right there."

"No, stay where you are," Roz replied, a playful note in her voice. "And close your eyes."

Sadie's smile widened as she dutifully closed her eyes and then turned toward the open door that led from the backroom into the Antique Mine. "My eyes are closed."

She could hear the shuffle of Roz's footsteps across the shop's hardwood floor. The aroma of boiled linseed oil hung in the air as she waited to see what Roz was up to now.

"Okay," Roz said, "take a look!"

Sadie opened her eyes and saw Roz standing in front of her, sporting a bright, white ski jacket with pink piping at the pockets and collar. But it was the white knit hat she wore, topped with two furry, white rabbit ears sticking straight up, that made Sadie laugh out loud.

"What in the world is on your head?" Sadie exclaimed.

Roz laughed with her, then did a graceful twirl on the toes of her sixties-era, white, patent-leather boots so that Sadie could view the outfit from all sides. "I'm going for the snow bunny look."

"And I'd say you've succeeded," Sadie told her. "Where did you find the bunny ears hat?"

"Believe it or not, I discovered it in a trunk in my basement." Roz's brown eyes flashed with amusement. "The trunk was full of the boys' old costumes from their school plays." She plucked the hat off her head and then used her fingers to tame her shoulder-length gray hair. "Randy wore this when he played the rabbit in the senior class production of *Harvey*."

Sadie nodded. "I remember that play. I just can't believe you kept his costume all these years."

Roz looked at the bunny hat in her hands. "It's one of those things you think might come in handy someday." Then she smiled at Sadie. "And it only took forty years to prove me right!"

Sadie chuckled.

"Are you planning to wear that bunny hat to the ski resort on Saturday? I can't wait to see Roscoe's reaction if you hit the slopes wearing those bunny ears."

"I know…" Roz's voice trailed off as she stared at Sadie. "Wait just one minute there, girl! Does that mean you're going to the Sneak Peek Saturday at Marwicke Manor?"

"It sure does," Sadie said with a grin. "I just got my invite yesterday." She walked over to a small table in the corner and picked up the invitation.

"*In appreciation of your donation to the Marwicke Manor Ski Resort,*" Sadie read out loud, "*we cordially invite you to join us for Sneak Peek Saturday: a day of skiing followed by a catered dinner. This event will take place on Saturday, January 24, beginning at one o'clock in the afternoon.*"

Roz clapped her hands together. "You actually did it! You finagled an invitation!"

Sadie nodded and then performed a little jig of celebration. Marwicke Manor and Ski Resort, located near Silver Peak, had been closed for almost forty years. Once an exclusive, private ski resort that had drawn celebrities and notable political figures from all over the country, the castle-style Victorian manor had sat empty for four decades, and then the ski resort closed.

The death of the owner, Paul Marwicke, in the 1977 avalanche, had shocked the small community of Silver Peak, although few residents had ever met him. Known as the hermit of Marwicke Manor, Paul had rarely left his home and had turned over the running of the ski resort to a contracting company. That contract had ended with Paul's tragic death and the place abandoned.

Just recently, to the surprise of everyone in Silver Peak, the opulent property had been sold to a man named Nolan Cross from Des Moines, Iowa.

While still residing in Iowa, the new owner had hired workers to restore the manor and ski resort area to full operation. The whole thing had been very hush-hush, which meant the entire town was talking about it.

"*Finagle* might be a strong word," Sadie said, feeling a little smug. "When I heard that the new owner was inviting people who had been involved in the remodel—like Roscoe giving Mr. Cross a discount at the hardware store—I figured I might as well give it a try." She pointed to the vintage wooden skis on the counter. "That's why I've been working so hard to get these restored in time. I bought them at an estate sale in Boulder a few years ago, but simply haven't had the time to restore them until now. I thought they'd make part of a nice vintage display at Marwicke Manor, so I ran the idea by Jeanne Sweeting and she agreed."

Jeanne, an event planner, had been hired by Nolan Cross to put together the Sneak Peek Saturday event for the reopening of the ski resort.

Roz grinned. "That's genius! And the skis look wonderful." Then she screwed up her nose. "They don't smell too wonderful though."

Sadie laughed "That's the boiled linseed oil and it is pretty pungent. It's a drying oil for paints and varnishes, but the smell will be gone by the time Jeanne picks up the skis and the rest of the display tomorrow afternoon."

Sadie walked toward the open doorway and then waited for Roz to leave the back room before she followed, closing the door behind them.

Roz took a seat at the counter on one of the tall stools while Sadie moved behind the counter and placed the Sneak Peek Saturday invitation inside her purse.

"I'm so happy you're going on Saturday." Roz unzipped her ski jacket as she settled onto the stool. "Now it will be twice as fun with both you and Edwin there!"

As the mayor of Silver Peak, Edwin had received an invitation just a few days after Sadie had called Jeanne and offered to donate the vintage snow skis, poles, and other antique ski equipment to display at the manor.

"I'm actually more excited about seeing Marwicke Manor than the skiing," Sadie confided, "given all the mystery surrounding the place."

"Me too," Roz said, leaning forward and resting her arms on top of the counter. "It's got a great gothic appeal, doesn't it? I mean first there was Deidre Marwicke, aka the mystery lady of Marwicke Manor. And then her son, Paul, the hermit of Marwicke Manor. The new owner could probably make a fortune just giving tours of the place."

Sadie nodded, hoping to learn more about the Marwicke family during the Sneak Peek Saturday. And get her first look *inside* the manor. It had been built in 1922 by Ernest and Viola Marwicke, Paul's paternal grandparents. Ernest Marwicke had been a Denver industrialist who had made his fortune buying mineral companies during the Colorado silver rush. Their only son, Frank, had married New York socialite Deirdre Boyd, the daughter of a wealthy family from New York City. Frank and Deidre had moved to the manor in 1928, so Frank could help his father run the exclusive ski resort that was the hot spot for celebrities of that era.

"I wonder why Paul never left the manor after his parents passed away," Roz mused. "He was still a young man. I know people used to say the Marwickes were too hoity-toity to rub shoulders with folks in town but...who knows? Paul must have been so lonely."

"Well, we know Paul *did* leave the manor on that awful day in 1977," Sadie said solemnly. "One of the few times the guy ventures outside of his enormous house and he's caught in an avalanche."

"They never found his body, did they?" Roz said, shaking her head. "That poor man."

In Sadie's mind, Paul Marwicke's life had been as much of a mystery as his death. The hermit of Marwicke Manor had hired others to run the ski resort after his parents had passed away, preferring to seclude himself inside his mansion. Although he'd lived near Silver Peak for all of his thirty-nine years, few townspeople had ever seen Paul Marwicke. His mother had homeschooled him and his father had presumably taught him to take over the family estate and business. Sadie wondered if his parents had ever imagined the solitary life their only child had chosen.

"Well," Roz said, breaking Sadie's reverie, "I guess it's time to go home and dig out our ski gear."

"How long has it been since you and Roscoe were on the slopes?"

"We went skiing about five years ago when Raleigh and his family were here for a visit," she said, referring to her younger son. "But I spent most of my time on the bunny slopes teaching my grandkids how to ski, so I'm excited to try some of the slopes at Marwicke."

"Me too," Sadie said with a smile. "And I need to break out my long underwear since the forecast will be cold with a chance of snow on Saturday."

"Even though it's supposed to snow, don't forget to bring sunscreen," Roz warned her. "You know how easy it is to get a sunburn on the slopes."

"Thanks for the reminder," Sadie said, making a mental note. "I'll pack it in my bag. You're taking along nice clothes for the dinner afterward, right?"

Roz nodded. "Yes, Jeanne told us we'd be given rooms to change out of our snow gear. I have a lovely maxi dress made of blue velvet and lace that should fit the ambiance of a place like Marwicke Manor. I just hope we have a chance to do a little exploring."

"Just think," Sadie said with a wistful sigh, "the manor's been frozen in time all of these years. And since it was built by Paul Marwicke's grandparents back in the 1920s, who knows what treasures we might find there?"

"Don't get your hopes up too high," Roz said with a smile. "Roscoe told me the new owner is a bit eccentric. When he delivered hardware supplies to the manor, Mr. Cross wouldn't even let him in the door."

"Well, Mr. Cross let Jeanne inside, and I heard Josh Ralston was part of a work crew doing some of the remodeling in the place. Maybe the new owner just wants to surprise everyone with a grand reveal."

"Maybe." Roz shrugged her shoulders. "Roscoe thinks Mr. Cross is an odd duck, but I guess we'll see for ourselves on Saturday."

Sadie couldn't wait. After forty years of sitting idle with all of its secrets hidden inside, Marwicke Manor was finally opening its doors again.